Gillian
BINCHY

Ruby's Tuesday

Published 2014
by Ward River Press.
123 Grange Hill, Baldoyle,
Dublin 13, Ireland
www.wardriverpress.com

© Gillian Binchy 2014

1

A catalogue record for this book is available from the British Library.

ISBN 978-1-78199-981-3

Printed by CPI Group (UK) Ltd, Croydon, CR0 4YY

www.wardriverpress.com

For our angel Zeldine

&

my gorgeous husband Gary

Prologue

They forgot to tell us that they were going to adjust the setting on the 21st of June 2013. That it would change from colour to black-and-white. Just like that, in the space of a few moments. That it would then be like watching a high-definition movie on a low-definition screen.

You see, before it happened we lived a happy, relatively stress-free life in high definition. The colours were sharp, the picture very clear and the sound a perfect pitch.

Then that day the sky and sea became a few shades duller. Never since have they been the same piercing blue as before. That shade of fierce cobalt blue you see on the Greek Islands or on a perfect summer day in Connemara – that indigo blue that makes you want to live overlooking Dublin Bay forever – well, on a sunny day, at least. Now that blue is more of a watery monochrome grey. Some days too, the sky and sea are just black with the odd speck of white.

Our life was now a telly that was a bit fuzzy, out of focus, just slightly imperfect.

The pain is a piercing ache in your heart that never goes away. It does dull a little with time, but it is there always like a lingering hangover, always in the background. On other days the agony is so brutal that it is debilitating.

Simple tasks are often difficult and overpowering. Reading instructions or directions is nearly impossible, because you can't concentrate – your mind flits in an instant. Comics with coloured pictures and word-bubbles are okay – they require less focus. Also, if you lose concentration, it has fewer consequences. You can just go back to the first coloured square on the top left-hand side of the page. And start again.

I imagine it must be like the onset of Alzheimer's; you lose your concentration and forget things. You are in a middle of a task and then you get lost. You get lost right there standing in your own kitchen, in a kitchen that has been yours for the last ten years, that you know every cubic inch of.

The secret, they say, is to manage the pain so that it becomes bearable, tolerable even. You need to lose your sense organs. You don't need them inside the newly fitted-out bubble – the bubble that has become your new life.

Sundays brought that dreaded feeling – like having to

go to work when the sun is out and everyone else is off. Digging sandcastles, enjoying creamy ninety-nines and sipping cool beers by the sea quickly became redundant hopes.

Now, I stay in on Sunday and sneak out into society during the week only when it is absolutely necessary – and to jog when I feel up to it. Once out there, I climb to the bubble. You see, in the bubble I can't hear screaming kids, I can't see perfect families, I can't taste freshly whipped full-fat wobbly ice-cream cones with oversized jagged chocolate flakes. Sun cream no longer smells of long hot days on a windswept beach. By shutting down the senses, I can block out all reminders of our lost future.

I wonder what they think at the local Sunday Farmers' Market – do they wonder what has happened to us? Did they have a good old gossip about us? More of a bitch than a gossip? Did they say that they always thought he was a bit odd, that he had a strange dark look about him, and that she always seemed a bit too giddy, like she was on something?

How could a couple who came to the local Farmers' Market every Sunday without fail, at the same time, after their morning sea swim, just stop coming? And no one had seen them since, not even on a single Sunday. Utterly bizarre, they would conclude. If he'd got a great new job and they were relocating, surely they would have come by to bid farewell to everyone, and wish them luck for the future? Wouldn't you expect that as a minimum, judging from their middle-class manners?

I wondered if the cheesemonger from Northern Spain would interrupt their gossip. Would she have enough broken English to defend us? Fabiana, the gorgeous little Catalan girl. Yes, she would defend us from their harsh words, of that I was sure – if they could understand what she was trying to tell them. Her kind and genteel nature would introduce some sympathy and sincerity into their argument. Her good-natured personality would shine through despite her fighting with the words.

Sunday was an event at which most of posh suburbia was doing happy shiny things, like showing off their well-educated kids by force-feeding them organic sushi from the market stalls. Then came the parade led by the toned and tanned husbands, as the wives looked on adoringly. They would call out gently, using sophisticated language to both the angelic kids and the equally well-trained pedigree Weimaraner. Middle-class suburbia put on a perfect performance for all to see. You were invited for just one day a week, a Sunday, to marvel at their wonderfully happy perfect tight-knit family units.

I declined their Sunday invitations. The market and its people became like other parts of my life, redundant, part of the past. I wished for fifty-two less Sundays in every year. Could I rename the day? Just ignore it, pretend that there were only six days in my newly invented calendar? After weeks of agonizing over a solution, I settled on the idea that my Sunday would become my Monday. Simple: I would stay in, do housework, read, watch TV on the Sabbath, thus avoiding a multitude of problems.

Sure, at first I missed the dark-green olives stuffed with creamy-coloured almonds; lunch was not the same without the warm crusty sea-salt-and-rosemary focaccia bread. A snack of carrots without basil hummus was not as tasty. But soon those familiar tempting tastes faded from my mind, until eventually I erased them completely. Such sensations were not allowed in the bubble, they were obsolete in the new version of reality.

Some Sundays, having worked from early morning until afternoon, as a late-lunch option I would down a bottle of chilled white wine, and munch on processed, farmed smoked salmon from the supermarket. Then, I would sleep the afternoon away, safely locked away from the happy perfect families. I would only rise when I was positive that it was well after all their bedtimes, when suburbia by the sea had emptied itself after the local performance.

So life went on . . . after a fashion.

Chapter 1

A Monday in July, 2013

I picked up my little girl and held her tight against my chest. She was very still.

"Ruby, my angel, your mum is off to run the pier. Be a good girl for your dad – he's in the other room, working – fighting with those bloody Chinese consultants. Be the best girl now till I get back. I will be only an hour, do you hear me? I love you, Ruby, my little angel."

I glanced back at her to make sure she was okay with the arrangement, but she didn't answer. How could she at her age? I tapped the fingers of my left hand gently onto my pink-glossed lips and blew my daughter a kiss.

"Bye, sweetheart, I'll be back very soon. Love you, Ruby."

Luke was on a conference call in the blue room, now temporarily his office. Gently, I opened the office door. He was slouched down in his office chair; they had beaten him down again, those tiresome Chinese clients. He didn't turn around to greet me.

I tippy-toed to the desk. I swung my head around to meet his face and planted a kiss on his forehead. He smiled gently, pointed to the phone then bobbed his middle finger up and down at it. Another day, I thought, that the friggin' Asians are getting the better of him.

I moved my arms up and down by my sides, to indicate that I was off for a run. In case he hadn't noticed my pink-and-black running outfit. He nodded and smiled at me. I rubbed the top of his back as I turned to leave and blew him a kiss but he didn't notice.

I closed the apartment door quietly – I didn't want to upset Luke or Ruby on my way out. I ran down the tattered carpeted stairs. The morning sunlight trickled through the red-and-yellow stained-glass window, landing on the carpet at the end of the stairs. I pulled the large yellow front door firmly shut behind me. I jogged down the wide granite steps, onto the loose gravel that groaned beneath my weight.

I was heading towards the green footbridge that would lead me to the sea front, and on to Dun Laoghaire's West Pier.

It was just after nine in the morning, the second last Monday in July.

There are two piers – one east and one west. They

look like giant arms stretching out in the sea – like they are hugging and holding the water, embracing it calmly, minding the water in their arms.

I always prefer the West Pier – or the 'poor pier' as I call it. It isn't perfectly paved like its sister pier. Also it is less busy there. The people that go there seem more real. At the end of the pier there is a single-storey lightkeeper's house. An enormous green lighthouse dwarfs it. People seem to come to this pier to work stuff out, judging by their thoughtful faces. I go there a lot. I find it very soothing to be on it.

The East Pier is the posh pier. It sells fancy coffee and homemade ice cream. It is where those perfect people in tight family units stroll. The tourists go there and couples on dates wander along it too. I'm always amazed how people having affairs brazenly walk up and down it, in public – walking down the pier with someone else's husband or wife. Confident young adults rollerblade along it, while spotty youngsters tormented by puberty and parents, skateboard on it, oblivious to everyone else.

It gets very busy, the East Pier; that is one of the reasons I don't go there any more. There are lots of buggies of every design, shape and size on it. Some are running ones, some single and more are double buggies.

A cyclist with thin hairy brown legs and a boney arse whizzed past me as I crossed over the green footbridge. He missed me only by inches and screamed some obscenity at me as he flew off in a blaze of luminous yellow.

I just shook my head and raised my eyes to heaven. Fixing my sunglasses on the top of my head, I jogged on.

A man wearing a chocolate-brown uniform was standing on the other side of the bridge, staring after the cyclist. "Near miss there!" he called out to me when I neared him.

"Yeah!" I replied, slowing down.

"That bloody cyclist nearly wiped you out!"

The man in the brown uniform seemed a bit too irate by my reckoning.

"Oh yes, he did, didn't he?" I responded calmly and stopped jogging. "Happens all the time – a cycle and running track together – 'tis madness – I've seen loads of collisions."

"Are you from around here – I mean, do you live nearby?" the man enquired.

I looked from his face to his jumper. On the left-hand side of the jumper was a burnt-orange-coloured emblem that announced itself as Swift Delivery.

"Well, yes, I live down the street, back there." I pointed in the direction I had come from.

"I'm looking for Coliemore Close – have you any idea where it is? I've been up and down every bloody street and alleyway and not a sign of it."

He had a distinct Dublin accent, and it had a familiar ring to it. I was suddenly afraid.

"Coliemore Close, Coliemore Close," I repeated, trying to sound normal and composed. "We live on Coliemore Road, so it must be somewhere around here."

His body froze. He appeared terrified by my words and looked almost shell-shocked. The man in brown, he didn't move an inch.

My heart sank; it felt like it might land on the ground in front of me. I felt sick. I started to shake from the inside out. I squeezed my left fist, dug my polished nails deep into the palm of my hand, swallowed very hard and fixed my gaze on two sandstone-coloured chimney pots just above the man's head. Then I took a deep breath.

I stood there for what felt like hours, rattling my mind to try to find words – any words would do – I just needed to say something.

And he stood too, gaping at me.

I was first to regain my composure.

"Have you delivered to Coliemore Road recently?" I enquired gingerly.

"Yes, yes, a couple of weeks ago. Jaysus, it must be nearly a month ago at this stage – 'twas a Friday afternoon during the heat wave, there in July. 'Twas a strange day, an unusual delivery."

"Are you Michael? Michael from Swift Delivery?" It must have seemed a stupid thing to say, a silly question, as his badge clearly read *Michael Thompson*.

"Yes," he responded. "I am Michael."

We stood looking at each other. A deadly silence hung between us. I stared and stared at him in disbelief.

"I am Afric. The girl you spoke to on the phone," I said, surprising myself with my efficient tones. "Do you remember me from that Friday a few weeks ago? The express delivery that you made to the large yellow door?" I took a step closer to him, maybe to assure him that it was okay.

"Jaysus, yes, of course, of course I do."

There was a standoff. Neither of us moved.

"Afric, I am so bloody sorry for you, for you both – my heart breaks for you. Life can be so bloody cruel. I hope that you're okay now – now that you're all together again . . . are ye okay?"

I could see that his eyes were wishing me to say yes, that we were okay.

"We're fine, it will be fine in the end, thanks," I replied. "I am so, so sorry for messing up your day. I felt so bad for you. I hope that I didn't upset you too much? But, look, I know I completely fecked up your weekend."

"Jaysus, Afric, don't be mad," he said. "I went home to the missus and told her what happened. I had her in floods of tears, and then of course she asked me what I said to you and I told her – Jaysus, she nearly killed me! 'What did you go asking her that for?' she growled at me."

We smiled a half smile at each other.

"I'm so sorry for asking – for asking what happened to her," he went on, "but sure you know men don't have a clue what to say in those circumstances, not a clue, but you know that I meant well – Jaysus, you do know that, don't you? God, life can be very cruel – I'm real sorry, missus, sorry for your trouble."

I could see that I had messed up yet another day in this stranger's life.

"Yes, it can be unkind," I said, "but I guess you have to take the bad with the good, don't you?" What else could I say? I took my shades from the top of my head and placed them over my eyes to conceal them, and to block out the July sunshine too. "Please tell your missus that I'm fine, that we are all fine. Thank you, Michael, for being so kind." I paused and carefully considered my words before going on. "Can I ask you something? Do you ever wonder what is inside all those boxes you deliver?"

He paused for a moment, as though searching for the answer I wanted to hear.

"Well, to be honest – not before that Friday – no, I never did, I never thought about it really. I suppose I just considered delivering boxes as 'the job' – it was just a job, like any other." He took a breath as if to steady his voice. "Now, it's different. I look at each box and wonder if what I'm delivering might change someone's life – will what I deliver make them happy or sad, am I good or bad news? But that's just for now – I'm sure that soon I'll deliver boxes like before, not thinking about it."

But I doubted this was the case. I was sure that the man with the chocolate-brown uniform would always wonder about the contents of every single delivery.

We parted company, with Michael still unable to locate Coliemore Close. Mind you, I hadn't been of much assistance to him.

13

I took off jogging towards the West Pier. I looked over my shoulder and saw a grown man in a dark-brown uniform reach into the left-hand pocket of his trousers for a handkerchief. He quickly wiped his eyes and put his sunglasses on.

This was the second day in his life that a girl with a strange name had ruined.

The perspiration ran off me. It was just after ten in the morning in late July and it was already a tropical twenty-three degrees outside.

I ran along the West Pier, the uneven surface of the breakwater grunting as I pounded down it and out towards the sea. A gentle breeze had attracted early-morning kite-surfers onto the large sandy patch of Shelley Banks. I could see the outline of their coloured sails to my left, off out in the distance. The reds and yellows stood out against the powder-blue sea. Flashes of dwarf furze cheered up the sea and sky with its fierce yellow colour. The furze too seemed a little duller this year. Maybe it was just that the morning heat haze had robbed the colour from the sea, sky and gorse?

To my right, young kids in oversized wetsuits were poured into life jackets too small for them. They were being tipped over by multicoloured toy boats, and their squeals reverberated between the two piers.

I pushed open the large yellow door and tippy-toed into the apartment, not wanting to disturb my husband and daughter.

I put my left ear up to the door of Luke's office. I wondered if he had finished that conference call to China.

For the eighteen months prior to the last week in June, when we had at last made vital changes to our life, I had tried to understand things from Luke's perspective. He did only have a few years to make it as a junior partner. It was a competitive world in international consultancy and even more cut-throat since the economy had slowed down. The demise of the Celtic Tiger had affected the whole country. I understood the long hours, the many international conferences that he needed to attend and speak at. Any decent wife would have been very proud of her husband for creating such a profile for himself in such a short time.

Of course I understood the importance of winning international clients, the significance of bringing in new international business, fresh business from outside of Ireland. That type of business was deemed more valuable, bringing new money into the country. It added weight to the sluggish economy; it was not the recycling of existing revenue.

Luke's role as Head of International Business Development had turned our lives upside-down. He had been away more than he was home for those eighteen months. At the start he was insistent that it was only for the first six months: as soon as he had his legs under the table then things would improve, or so he said – there would be less travelling and we would return to normal.

Back then Luke would try to spend hours explaining all the whys to me. It was not that I didn't understand it, I did of course, but the result was still the same: Luke was never home.

We were now living the new 'normal' married life that we had adjusted to since that last week in June. Luke no longer travelled and I had taken the summer off work. I thought at first I would have difficulty adapting to the new version of our marriage, where we were literally together twenty-four hours a day – but no. Surprisingly not. We seemed to enjoy each other's company again, maybe because we had spent so much time apart over the past eighteen months. We were beginning to work out a routine, though with parameters. Our sex life was back on track, evenings were spent sea-swimming in our old spots, and we were ticking over, just about.

I had always felt guilty, well, mildly anyway, that Luke worked day and night, literally, when he was doing all that travelling. Since the promotion all that had changed. Now he was working from home until they set him up in his new office with a river view of the Liffey, one of the rewards for the gruelling eighteen months toiling in the Chinese market. It would be ready, they said, in another few weeks, so the commuting would begin again, but nothing compared to the weekly commutes to China.

My job, on the other hand, was a means to an end. It was grand, just about. I went to the office day in day out and managed a bunch of people that were unmanageable in an IT company. I had kind of resigned myself to it about a year ago, when the managing director, who was even more trying than my team, refused to confront the multitude of issues that stood in the way of increasing the profit margin. Obsolete technology and systems, and a poorly trained team, low staff moral and zero investment in innovation meant that the company limped from one unstable contract to another. The pay was average, but the terms and conditions were good, and they had looked after me very well this summer when I needed to take a few months off. So I would stick it out. It suited me, and I sort of suited them.

"Imagine working in a technology company – even worse, being a manager – and not having a smart phone!" I would say to Luke.

Luke would tease me and say: "Gorgeous, there's a call for you!"

I would rush from our bedroom, from the desk at the window overlooking the sea, to my old Nokia brick that was permanently charging at the wall in the living room.

He would giggle and say: "It's the cavemen – they're looking for their phone back."

I would fall for his silly joke, every time. Sometimes, annoyed with myself, I would deliver him one of my frostier dirty looks and go back to my desk with the view of the sea, back to my book.

For a while I would ignore his advances and apologies, I would block him out, pretend for just a few minutes that he no longer existed. He would tiptoe into our bedroom and stand by my desk and tell me to give him a hug. I would for a few moments ignore him, dismiss him, just to tease him, as if reprimanding a bold child for its bad behaviour. Then, he would get scared that I might be cross with him. He didn't like it if I was even just a little bit upset. In his head he had the idea of a perfect relationship. That was what he lived for: perfection.

He would retreat – go back to his office. Then I would give in and get up from my chair by the window and meet him halfway in the living room and run into his open arms, into his chest. I would lay my head on his chest. There it was safe, and there the hurt would disappear, if only for a few seconds or even for a moment – that was all we could ask for now.

When I teased him and he got upset, I was unable to watch the sadness that descended over his puppy eyes. The only thing I dreaded was that the melancholy would tumble down over those chocolate-brown eyes, like a mist coming in over Dublin Bay. His eyes would then resemble the bay on days when it looked vacant, monochrome and without life. His change of mood, like the mist, could happen in a matter of minutes.

Now, as I listened from outside the door, I could no longer hear Luke's tender tones inside the blue room – but he had a soft voice so I wasn't sure if he was on the phone to those bloody clients or not.

Very slowly, I opened the door.

"Sweetheart . . . Luke?" I whispered

I waited for him to respond, to turn around and acknowledge my presence.

"Luke, can I talk to you for a second?" I asked in a low focused voice.

I wanted to make sure that I was not breaking his concentration. Luke was a very focused type of person, and very organized, and he disliked intensely being interrupted. I constantly teased him about his inability to multitask. He never did deny how challenging he found it. I'd had to constantly remind myself for the past month that we had not in a long time spent so much time together. Living in such close quarters needed guidelines and parameters, and with those it would be fine.

"Yes, Afric, what's up?"

By his tone I knew to keep it short. We were not here for a casual chat. I was only invited to talk business or for 'information exchange', as I had termed it in the last few weeks.

One of the reasons that Luke had been so successful in the Chinese market place was that he never got sidetracked, and though the Chinese were willing to waste hours on unimportant details of a contract, this never distracted Luke. Out of courtesy, he would allow them to waffle on for hours on end. Calmly, he would always bring them back, back to the important issues. The contracts that Luke signed with the Chinese were one-hundred-per-cent watertight. About the Chinese he would say: "It's all about attention to detail – all the i's need to be dotted, otherwise they would wiggle out of a contract when it suited them, and Sheppard Consulting and I would be left holding the baby."

Luke was Sheppard Consulting's golden boy.

"No, nothing important, sweetheart – just about the arrangement for the weekend," I replied efficiently, in case he thought I was lingering in his space and on his time. I had become over-efficient since he had moved his office back into the apartment.

"Yes?" he responded.

"Well, what time do you want us to leave this afternoon, for the airport?"

There was silence. He swung his chair away from me and towards the window. He lifted up the white net curtain and looked out onto the road below where the traffic whizzed up and down Coliemore Road.

"God, Afric, I wouldn't have a clue. It's over a month now since I've been to an airport – a full month, can you believe it? Isn't that fantastic?" He seemed radiant. "Almost five bloody weeks since I've been in an airport." He swung his chair around again and looked directly at me. "What time do you think, Afric? Whatever you think – you have a better idea of the traffic on a Friday than I do."

"Would about four suit you?" I was genuinely surprised to be allowed such air time.

He shrugged his shoulders. "I'm happy to do whatever you think."

"Yes, four should be plenty time. That will give us enough time to drop Ruby off on the way." My tone was now even more efficient as I felt as though I was on his borrowed time.

"I thought you told me that Sue was coming to pick her up?" he replied in a deadpan voice.

"Sure it's miles out of her way – and anyway we're heading that direction to the airport."

He looked at me with a slight grimace, so that his clusters of summer freckles were even closer to each other than normal. They were so close, I was afraid they might increase and multiply.

"Luke, I'd be happier if we could drop her off. I'd feel better if we could settle her in, see where she's staying, make sure the room is okay. I'd be more relaxed then about leaving her. Is that okay?" But I was determined to get my way.

Luke got up from the desk and walked around to where I stood, in the middle of his office. His opened his arms and drew me into his solid chest.

"Of course, my sweetheart, it is. Of course you're right. We'll both be happier if we know that she's okay when we're away." He caressed the top of my head, then ran his hand right down over my hair onto my back. "I know it's very tough leaving her for the first time – the first time is the worst and then, I promise you, it will be fine, all the other times will be fine – I promise you it will get easier. Let's concentrate on getting the first time out of the way and make it as easy for us all as possible. We must try not to get too upset." He held me tight, very tight. He rubbed my back tenderly and ran his hands up and down my arms. "Sweetheart, please don't worry, it will be fine. Have a hot shower and relax before we head off. Why don't you lie down for a few

21

hours, have a nap? You'll feel better after that, I promise you will."

I always felt okay when my head was placed on Luke's chest. I felt it was the safest place on the planet. There, snuggled between his arms, nothing or no one could hurt me. For the past couple of weeks, it was the only place where I found solace.

My body craved his; I wanted to lie down beside him, with my cheek placed on his firm hairy chest. Sometimes, when I drifted off to sleep on his chest, I would wake up coughing when his chest-hairs had crept up my nose and tickled the membranes inside. Then Luke would rub the side of my forehead very gently, to settle me again. He would caress my face until I drifted off again, then later, somehow, some time, when I was fast asleep, he would extract himself from underneath my needy body and try to carve out some bed space for himself for just a few hours . . . until I searched once again for the safest place in the world, between his arms, on his chest.

Every morning, when I woke up beside, instead of on, his chest, I felt cheated. I would stretch out my hand, look for the matted hair and crawl back on to his chest, into his arms. Gently, I would rub his chest in a circular motion, to remind him I was there, in case he hadn't noticed.

"Shh, Afric, shh, my sweetheart," he whispered now. "It will be fine, she will be fine with Sue, with her godmother . . ." His voice trailed off as he rubbed the top of my head gently and caressed the side of my face.

"I know, I know, you're right. I'm fine, honestly, I'm grand. I'll feel better when she's properly settled into Sue's house. Sue will look after her really well and anyway, sure, she's a very low-maintenance child. Sue said she's looking forward to having her." I cleared my throat. I looked up and into his milk-chocolate eyes. "I'm fine, really I am. I'm going to go and pack now for both of us."

"Afric, I love you, you are my world. Please don't be upset – it's only for two sleeps that she's going to stay with Sue. Two sleeps only and then we'll be back."

I didn't want to disturb him any further, so I turned to walk to the door

"Afric . . . Afric!" The second Afric was louder than the first.

I turned back and waited.

"Sweetheart, if you get very, very sad, we can always come home," he said, walking towards me. "There are loads of flights from London every day. We'll just jump on the next plane and come home. We can be back home with her in a matter of hours." He cupped my face in his hands, then with his index finger he traced my lips, first the bottom lip and then the top one. "Afric, I love you. Whatever will make you happy, whatever it is, we will do." He tapped me gently on the bum, as if dismissing me, now that he had heard my plea.

"Thanks, Luke, I love you." I left his arms and walked to the door, then looked back and gave him a quarter of a smile; it was more of a gesture than a smile. I pulled the door of his new office gently closed behind me.

I walked into the room where my daughter was. She had not moved from where I left her before my run down the pier.

"Ruby, my sweetheart, Mummy's back from her jog on the pier. It's a beautiful morning out there. We have the first heat wave in years and your mummy is roasting."

I picked up my little girl and kissed her tenderly.

"Ruby, I am so happy to have your dad back. Yes, my little girl, your daddy is back now from China and he will never have to go back there again. Isn't that so good, my little angel?" I rubbed her very gently. "And, guess what, your dad is happy – well, as happy as can be expected – he seems very happy to be back home with you and me. Isn't it great that we're all together again? Ruby, I am so glad that you are here with us, that you're back home with your mum and dad." I kissed her again. "Now there's something I need to tell you. My little angel, your mum and dad are going to head off for the weekend. We're only going for two nights, so you're going to stay with your godmother, your Fairy Godmother Sue. You're going to Sue's house and she will look after you. Do you hear me? My little girl, you're going on your holidays too, like your mum and dad, except we're going to different places, not together this time. You're going to the Northside of Dublin for your holidays. Then on Sunday morning Mum and Dad will come and collect you and bring you back home safe and sound. Is that okay?"

Ruby as yet didn't have words, so she could not speak, and I had developed this awfully rude habit of talking for her and at her.

"Ruby, don't you know that your mum will miss you lots and lots? I'll be very sad leaving you for the first time, but Mummy has promised Dad that she will not cry. So, my little angel, you are to be good until I come back. Do you hear me, my little angel? Ruby, do you hear your mummy?"

There was no response.

"Afric! Afric!" Luke hollered from his office. He came hurrying out with my phone in his hand. "Afric – there's a missed call from Sue – you left your phone in my office."

I redialled the last missed call.

"Sorry, Sue, I missed you, I'm just in the door," I wittered down the phone. "I was on the pier, went for a run, trying to get rid of some of those bloody pregnancy pounds – Jesus, Sue, they're nearly impossible to shift –"

"Afric, don't be ridiculous, no one but yourself even notices them. It's all in your head!"

"I wish, Sue. It's not in my head, I wish it was – it's on the scales and, as we both know, the scales don't lie!" I giggled.

"You know, the white wine adds the pounds on too . . ."

"Fuck off, Sue," I said jokingly, clearly pronouncing each word. "Fuck off – don't you start!"

"Afric, don't be so hard on yourself. Sure it's only a month since you gave birth to Ruby. It takes weeks, months and even years to shift those bloody pounds. I still haven't got rid of all the weight after the twins and they are nearly six – it takes time for your metabolism to readjust." She paused. "Well, maybe not six years, that's the extreme, but, God, give yourself a break, honestly, after all you've been through."

"God, Sue, it feels like months ago since I gave birth," I said, my voice beginning to tremble.

"That's a good sign, Afric, very good. It means that you're moving in the right direction, moving forward, getting back on track . . . Afric, what was it I wanted to say to you? Oh, back to Ruby – just checking in with you on the arrangement for me to collect her – I said I'd give you a quick call to see what suited. Do you want me to come by and collect her soon? That would probably be easier for you. Both the boys are on play dates so I'm free now, and if you had the time we could have a coffee in the sunshine down by the pier."

"Don't be mad," I replied. "Sure we have to go to the airport anyway so we'll be out your direction, so how about we drop her off and then head straight for the airport? Honestly, Sue, we'll drop Ruby off. I don't want to put you out, especially when you're so kind as to have her for a few nights. Would about five this afternoon suit?"

"Okay so . . . if you're sure . . ."

"I am."

"Right – see you about five. Love to Luke!"

And she was gone.

I tugged the silver zip around the corner of the blue carry-on case. I looked up at our daughter, from where I sat in the middle of the bedroom floor. My head felt a little dizzy as I stood up.

"Oh Ruby, your mum has a little pain in her head today – a few glasses of wine too many last night. Your dad says your mum is a lush but don't mind him – that's not true. Your mum is not a lush, sure she's not? Do you know what a lush is, sweetheart?"

But of course she couldn't speak.

"I will tell you, Ruby," I said. "A lush, according to your daddy, is your mum, but I tell him not to worry – that I have a whole six months of partying to catch up on. Do you know what he says? He says surely by now I must have made up that time. Do you know what I say? I say, no, I have another five months of white wine to drink. I have only drunk a month so far. He normally raises his eyes to heaven and goes back to his office then."

I walked closer to our daughter, hoping that she might hear better and pay more attention to me. She seemed to have no interest in my trivial conversation. Well, I suppose it was not a conversation – it was more like one-way traffic, me speaking at her – and she could not run away from me, not at her age.

"Ruby, my little girl, you're starting early – ignoring your mother when she's speaking to you!"

I was sure she was thinking: There's Mum ranting on again.

"Right, Ruby, hope that you're ready for your little break, off to the Northside to your Fairy Godmother. I spoke to her just now and she's looking forward to having you. I told her you would be no bother, so please, Ruby, be good for her. You'll have plenty company – Jack and Frankie will be there – I know they're a bit wild, but it's just their age. I know you would never be like them, so I'm not worried that you'll pick up any of their bad behaviour. Ruby, it will be nice for a change to have other kids around – it will be good for you to have other kids for company – and, anyway, it is nice too to have a change of scene – sometimes we all need a change of scene."

Luke popped his head around the door. "Are you still talking at your poor daughter?"

I smiled but didn't answer. Sometimes I forgot how loud I was when I was talking to Ruby. Other times, I completely forgot that Luke was in the house.

"Are you ready to go in ten minutes, sweetheart?" Luke spoke only to me.

"That's perfect – nearly ready – I just need to get Ruby's stuff together then I'm ready for the off."

He ignored my comment.

"I'll take Ruby down to the car if you can take the luggage," I said.

He just smiled and left the room. His milk-chocolate eyes looked like that haze might come again. I hoped not, not this weekend anyway.

"We're off in ten minutes, my little angel. Mummy just needs to get your blanket, to wrap you up, to keep you safe on the way to Sue's and so that you are warm enough in her house."

I wrapped her safely in a multicoloured blanket, the one that her grandmother Lizzy had got for her before she was born.

"Luke, see you downstairs! I have Ruby!" I called out from the living room.

"Okay, love," his chirped from his office.

I thought his voice sounded rather upbeat under the circumstances.

"My gorgeous girl, we are ready – let's go – we're all off on our holidays, your dad and I and you too."

I picked up my little girl in her blanket and cradled her in my left arm. I held her tight against my chest, careful not to drop her. Slowly, very slowly, I walked down the frayed steps that led from the apartment to the front door. Carefully I secured each foot before moving the next – I was so paranoid about dropping my precious cargo.

Luke thundered down the stairs behind me with the luggage and held the heavy yellow door open for me and Ruby. I walked out and down the wide granite steps onto the gravel that led to the black gate.

"Luke?" I looked over the roof of the car at him.

"Yes, my love?"

"I'll sit with Ruby in the back, to keep her company. Is that okay?" I asked, almost as if seeking permission.

"Of course, sweetheart, whatever makes you happy." His tone was low.

He turned on the ignition of the car, his car.

I whispered to my little girl: "Say goodbye to the apartment, Ruby. Tell it we'll be back home soon, all three of us – only two sleeps and we'll be back together again, back home safe behind the yellow door. Go on, Ruby, blow a kiss to the house – tell it we'll be home in two sleeps – blow it a kiss, Ruby. Just two more sleeps and I'll be with you again."

I lowered the window gently and, bringing my fingers up to meet my lips, I blew hard at our apartment.

"Bye, house, bye, see you soon!" I waved at the yellow door.

Luke looked at me in the rear-view mirror. He said nothing.

We sat there in the back of the car; I sat on the left and Ruby on the right. She was all wrapped up in the multicoloured blanket. I reached across and fastened her seat belt. I opened the top of the blanket so that she would have a better view on the way to her godmother's. I raised the window, leaving it just a little open on my side, to give us both some air.

We would drive along the coast road, all along the coast road, the road that Ruby and I had travelled the day we were on the way to the maternity hospital, before she was born.

Sue's house was further along that drive, past the airport, nearer to Howth, not too far from Howth lighthouse – the grey-and-white Baily lighthouse. I felt more comfortable knowing that Ruby would be in familiar surroundings, near the lighthouse – it was the same lighthouse that she could see from the desk of our bedroom window. She would have a view of it from Sue's house, a different view, but she would still be able to see it. From the window in Sue's house, she would have a great view of the east and west piers too – she'd be able to see the red and green lighthouses though she'd be looking at them from the opposite side of Dublin Bay. But they were still familiar surroundings for Ruby. It would take her no time to settle in there.

Luke switched on the radio. It was just four o'clock, and time for the afternoon news.

"Ruby, do you remember the day that you and I drove past here and I told you all the stories? Only a few weeks ago when you and I were on the way to the maternity hospital? Sweetheart, Mummy is talking to you – do you remember?"

Ruby was silent. Luke was too.

The heat of the July afternoon and the motion of the car lulled me off to sleep.

When I woke up I saw Luke glance into the rear-view mirror.

"Luke," I piped up, "sorry I fell asleep. I'm wrecked from the run this morning."

He didn't mention the wine last night, nor did I.

"We're almost there," Luke announced. "Which house is it? I can never remember – there are so many bloody laneways around here."

"Sue's house is the grey one there, with the red

windows – yes, that one just to the left."

It was one of the few occasions that Luke was willing to take instructions when driving.

"Ruby, we're here at last at your godmother's, your Fairy Godmother's. See there at the door – there's Sue – do you see her? There waiting for you. Ruby, give her a wave, a big wave."

I waved frantically at Sue for both of us. I opened Ruby's seat belt and fixed her so that she was properly wrapped in her multicoloured blanket. I wanted her looking well for her godmother.

Then I picked her up, got out of the backseat, and we hurried to greet Sue.

"Hi, hon! Lovely to see you!" Sue chirped.

She gave me a big hug; it was so tight that I was afraid I might drop Ruby.

"You too." I gave her a big kiss on the cheek.

"Luke, so good to see you," said Sue, "and congratulations on being back on this side of the world. You must be thrilled?"

"Sue, I can't tell you how relieved I am," said Luke. "It's a month now and I hardly know myself . . ." He paused. "I mean, we're doing okay, as well as could be expected."

He looked at me, to confirm it was true, that we were doing okay. My mouth smiled at him; my eyes didn't move much.

"You are so good to mind Ruby for us – we both really appreciate it," I said.

"Sure she's no trouble at all and there's no minding her. Isn't that what Fairy Godmothers are for anyway? Come in, come in for a bit." She opened the door to the house.

Jack and Frankie came running out of the living room to the front door.

"Mummy, Mummy, can we meet Ruby? Can we meet Ruby?" Jack squealed.

"Jack, Jack, what did I tell you earlier – what did Mummy say to you about Ruby?"

Jack hesitated. "You said that she was very very small, only a baby, and that she was not made like me and Frankie – she's too young to play – her body is too young to play – and that all she does is sleep all the time."

Sue pointed in the direction of the back garden. "Now, say hello to Luke and Afric and then go out to the back garden."

"Hello, Afric, hello, Luke," the twins chimed in chorus.

They were gone.

Digging my nails deep into my right hand, I took a long breath and looked away. I looked ahead at a picture – I have no idea what the picture was of. I counted very slowly to five. I stood there inside the door, frozen, there in the hall. I realised that my little Ruby would never play like the twins.

I looked at Luke, checking to see was that dreaded mist rolling into his eyes. He winked at me and smiled, and I knew we would be okay.

"Sue, we won't stay long as we have a few things to get in the airport, so if it's okay I'll settle Ruby upstairs and we'll make tracks straight away."

Somehow, I managed to get the entire sentence out.

"You know which room is hers, don't you? The dormer room upstairs, the room with the sea view of the three lighthouses. She's safest up there away from the boys. Go on up and settle her, the two of you, but make sure that you lock the door on the way out – and you'd better bring the key down here to me – I don't want the twins up there meddling with her." She indicated to us to go upstairs.

Slowly and carefully I climbed up, careful not to drop our little girl on the winding wooden stairs.

"Are you okay there, Afric?" Luke enquired. He rubbed the bottom of my back as I climbed the stairs in front of him.

"Yes, sweetheart, I am fine, just fine," I replied. I steadied my voice. "Now, Ruby, let's go and have a look at your room. Your Fairy Godmother gave you the best room in the house. Aren't you the lucky girl? Look there, look out the window – can you see three lighthouses? The same three lighthouses you can see from our house. Look at the green lighthouse in the distance – that is near your house, where you live, so don't be lonely. Sue will take care of you, Mummy and Daddy will be back home soon – only two sleeps and we'll be back to collect you." I rubbed her very gently.

Luke walked from the window back to the centre of the room where I stood holding our little girl. He opened his arms, wider than normal to welcome both of us into them, to a place where we both could be safe, and there in his arms nothing more could happen to his girls. He held us tight, all three of us locked together in heartache. Then he dropped his head down and kissed me on the top of my head very softly, so that I could feel the warmth of his breath on my forehead. Then very slowly he opened the blanket and leant in and kissed his tiny little girl.

"Love you, Ruby. I'll miss you very much, my little girl," he whispered to her. "I'll be back soon to collect you, to take you back into my arms, to take you home again."

Ruby seemed completely oblivious of her parents' departure.

Chapter 2

One Month Before . . .

A Friday in June, 2013

Her hazel-green eyes almost popped out of her skull and onto the computer screen. Her concentration was fierce. I strained my neck to the right to see what she was looking at. She tilted the screen ever so slightly away from the examination bed, and moved it closer to her. She was like a greedy child, wanting it only for herself.

Mary glanced briefly at me, but her eyes didn't meet mine. Mine tried to flirt with hers, to attract them, but she was careful to avoid contact.

A large flat plasma screen occupied some of the cream wall; it was positioned right in front of me and directly behind Mary's head. She didn't look at the large screen, my screen, but instead concentrated on her monitor, the smaller one.

I lay there on the flat of my back, like a kid waiting for a movie to start, but for some reason there seemed to be a delay. However, the screen and the lady failed to announce what the setback might be. I thought it best to wait patiently; I didn't want to distract the lady with the green eyes.

Then an image of something moving popped up on the big screen. The thing displayed in black-and-white seemed tiny on the vast wall-screen. I wondered how something so tiny could have all that energy and move so frantically. What was its hurry? Where was it going in such a rush?

On the bottom right-hand side of the screen, displayed in dark-red writing, was a type of an announcement that read: **Client: Afric Lynch DOB: 11/11/72**.

I moved my head forward, trying to get closer to that screen. The thing, it kept moving, and the monitor said that this frantic thing was mine. But Mary still wanted the screen just for herself. But it was mine, not hers – not the screen, I mean, but the thing that moved on the screen. I was going to be a mother. Of course I could do this, I told myself. Yes, I could do this – I could be a mother and put this blob, right there on the screen, first. Well, the blob would develop a little more and become a person, eventually. I could give up everything: the long-distance sea-swimming, the wild camping holidays to exotic places. I could even sacrifice the boozy weekends away with the girls.

Those inklings that had been troubling me were now in a small dark corner of my head, and there they must stay, forever, safely tucked away. Those people were right, the ones who told me that I was imagining things. They were correct, those sensible people when they told me to get a grip, that it was just the damned hormones. Take no notice, they said, just plough on. I did that.

Lying there flaked out on the bed, for the very first time ever I started to consider the long-term future. There it was in black-and-white on the screen. I was looking at our future: the baby's, mine and Luke's. This was the new version of our family. I could be a mother. I was sure that I could do it, that we together could work it out.

She pressed the cold grey hand-scanner into my flesh; skillfully, she used it to move the clear gunge around my midriff. Even though my baby was tiny, ever so tiny, the scanning seemed to take an eternity.

Mary was well organised, or so I thought – she had a list, like one you might take to the supermarket. Her process had a beginning, middle and an end. She had a record of the things that she needed to find. When Mary found something that she needed for her list, having located it she would then scan it, and then measure its dimensions, both length and width. Then she would call it out, very slowly, pronouncing the newly found item very clearly. She was as precise as those people on telly who call out the lottery-ball numbers.

Mary didn't address the names to me. They were called out for herself, and it was part of her process, like her own TV show. Then she would stick the name of whatever she had found up on the top right-hand corner of the large screen, my screen on the wall. Then, she would sit back on her chair and admire it proudly.

She didn't appear to make any connection between my body and the body on the screen.

I wondered how many things were on her list. Were we talking a hundred or just maybe ten? I toyed with the idea of asking, but decided against it. Her concentration was too fierce to interfere with.

So the well-organised shopper, Mary, continued with her list. It was hers because she didn't share it with me. What I didn't understand was why she didn't start with the baby's head or toes and work her way either up or down the body. Instead she had a bizarre approach: she started with the head, then headed off down the body looking for a spine, then back to the head, then all the way down again to the heart, and up again to the head. It didn't seem to me to be a good use of her or my time. All the time she stuck to the list and never deviated from it.

Mary was the type of lady you would never find in the special-offers section of the supermarket. She would only visit the aisles where she needed to be. She would know where every aisle was located and what item was on each shopping lane. If an item was not on the list, she would never dream of even putting a foot down its aisle. She would be every marketer's dream; she would score ten out of ten on brand loyalty. She would never purchase replacement items; she would do without and then return the following week at the same time and purchase the item that she had failed to secure the week before. She could wait to get the full list completed.

Mary cleared her throat and spoke very calmly. "Afric, the baby will have long legs, very long femurs, but then the femur is the longest bone in the body, isn't it?"

Was she asking me to agree with her or was she was not certain whether it was the longest bone in the body? Not sure of an appropriate reply, I just nodded.

That seemed to suit her fine.

"See the heart, there." She swung around on the chair and pointed her thin bony finger at the centre of the screen on the wall. "Just there pumping away good – well, you don't need to worry about the heart – your baby has very strong heart."

"Oh, yes, I see it right there. God, it's racing like hell," I replied, careful not to chatter on too much. I wondered if I was looking at the right bit, but I decided against enquiring.

"A baby's heart beats faster than ours – sometimes up to three times faster. Crazy, isn't it?" Then she repeated: "Your baby has a very strong heart."

I thought that she had done the heart – why had she not moved on to somewhere else? At this rate she would never finish her list, if she was back to the heart again.

Now I realise that maybe she was trying to give herself hope, hope that really it was only a matter of time until she found what she was looking for. What she was searching so desperately for.

"Your baby has a well-developed nose," she reported confidently. "At this stage we can tell if a baby has Down Syndrome by the shape of its nose."

My baby had a pointy nose, just like mine. I could see it on the screen. To be honest, it was the only thing I saw clearly, the nose I mean. The pounding heart I never did really recognise.

"A pointy nose is a good sign. When we see flat noses we are often in trouble. Anyway, all fine there."

Something about Mary had changed – her manner – she appeared to be a little less frosty, as if she was trying to built up confidence between us. Previously, she seemed only interested in the baby, but now she seemed keen to include me in the proceedings.

"That's good news, isn't it?" I replied. "My mum had a Down Syndrome sister. Her name was Yvonne. It would break your heart to watch her. Yvonne had an eating disorder, and so all the presses in my granny's house had locks so that she couldn't get at the food. My granny would put elastic bands on the packets of biscuits and crackers so that Yvonne couldn't open them. With Down's, you see, she would never be able to open the biscuits."

Mary appeared to be listening intently to me ranting on about something that I knew very little about. But she didn't interrupt me.

"I thought that very cruel, to tease someone like that," I rattled on. "It was like they were taking advantage of her, kind of fooling her. Well, it served them right, because then she would throw one of her epic tantrums – that was her revenge. And what was worse they'd given her a horrible name – imagine being called Yvonne – it even looks ugly on paper, and sounds worse when you pronounce it. Even to this day, I'm not that keen on biscuits."

"I see, I see, that is terrible, isn't it? Well, Afric, you don't have to worry about that – your baby is fine on that front."

Mary continued to race up and down the baby, moving from head to limb to heart but all the time returning to the head. She was scanning like crazy, though the list on the screen didn't seem to increase in proportion to the activity around my stomach.

"Afric, there might be a problem with the foot, with the left one. Look there – do you see how it is turned in? That in itself is nothing to worry about, nothing at all – it could be the way that it's lying in the womb." Mary dug the hand-piece of the ultrasound machine deep into my stomach and twisted it so that it dug into my bladder. "No," she said, "I still can't get the angle that I need to see the back of the head. Do you know if your baby is a boy or a girl?"

"No," I replied. "We said we'd wait until it was born."

This reply didn't seem to suit Mary.

"Why don't you walk around, have a glass of cold water? That might move your baby into a better position, and then I can get a better view of the back of the head."

"Okay," I said.

"Are you in any rush?" she asked me politely.

"No, not at all," I responded.

Mary excused herself from the room. I pulled down my black woollen top, zipped up my jeans and headed off for a walk . . . just around the room. I walked to one cream wall, turned around when I got there and then walked back to the wall on the opposite side of the room, from where I had started. In no time at all, I had a kind of a system going. I felt like a school kid who had been given an exercise to do while the teacher had left the classroom to use the bathroom. I decided it was best to keep walking around in case she came into the room and caught me not walking and scolded me. After all, we were getting on much better now, Mary and I, and I didn't want that to change . . .

Gently she opened the door and returned to her seat by the screen, the smaller screen.

"Right, pop up there again, Afric, and we'll have another look." Her right hand invited me to climb up onto the examination table.

So there I lay on the flat on my back, with my belly button peering up at the white ceiling while Mary searched desperately for something that she would never find. The way she spoke of it, I expected that the missing item might turn up somewhere daft like in the stomach or the liver. All the time she searched only for that one thing.

Determined, she repeatedly and desperately tried to get the right angle. She moved her petite body, craned her neck and twisted her head in a vain attempt to get the baby into the correct position. All she needed was the right position so that she could scan the back of the head. Again she moved quickly from one end of the baby's tiny body to another. She viciously dug the rounded metal scanner into my skin, without apology. Again she returned to the head, time and time again, each time a little more disappointed than the last. By now she was struggling to disguise her frustration.

Then she did get the baby's head in the correct position.

Mary was of course going to tell me that she had made a big mistake. She would say that she was having a bad day, that it was there all the time. I thought she might tell me that maybe she should have left work and gone home early, because that morning she had a terrible argument with her husband and was upset, and that she could not think clearly.

She might then say that it was the way that the baby was lying that made it very difficult to find the thing she was looking for. All she needed to say was: 'Your baby is perfect.' Then I would get off her examination table, and she could go home to her husband. Then we would both be happy. I would swear to never tell anyone about her mistake – it could be our secret. She just needed to say that everything was okay. But no. Time after time she took measurements of the skull, from every possible angle, top to bottom, side to side, side to bottom, top to side, front to back, back to front. By now I was starting to get very frustrated. How many bloody times did she need to measure the same item? Methodically, she repeated the exercise time and time again.

Now, it was just Mary and the blob on the screen. I had been excluded once again.

"I've seen enough, thanks, Afric," she muttered at last in a hushed tone. "I'm afraid your baby has an . . ." Then she spoke those two dread words: "*Absent cerebellum*."

She then committed them to paper.

Our report was just a single page. It was a light-green A4 sheet. It said that our baby had an absent cerebellum and had congenital talipes – that was the problem with the foot. There were other things too, but they were not as important.

Funny how one day you have never heard of the word *cerebellum* and within seconds it becomes the only focus of your life. Those blasted words *absent cerebellum* were now part of our future. It would be long time, if ever, that they would leave my mind.

She didn't find our baby's brain in its liver or stomach, and she never did put *cerebellum* up on the top right-hand corner of the screen, with the other words. And look proudly at it. Without those two words, her list was incomplete and superfluous.

She glanced at the second-last finger of my left hand. The evidence of a wedding ring seemed to be a relief to her.

"Afric, are you married – or do you have a partner?" she enquired tenderly.

"Yes, yes, I'm married to Luke, but he's in China at the moment," I replied cautiously.

"Do you want me to call someone for you – a friend maybe or relation? Is there someone that you would like to talk to now?" She seemed persistent again in the same way that she had been determined in trying to find the nonexistent cerebellum.

And what the hell was I going to say to them, I wondered. Would I say: 'Look here, this lady called Mary has spent the last two fucking hours looking for my baby's cerebellum. Do you have any bloody idea where it is, cos she clearly hasn't a bleedin' clue and this is meant to be her job? Is it any wonder that this country is the way it is? No doubt she's paid a friggin' fortune and she can't even scan my child. Any chance you can call her and give her a clue as to where the hell she might find it, because now she is pissing me right off?'

"Thanks but Luke's the one I'd like to talk to and he's in a different time zone, so I couldn't call him now – no, not Luke, not now . . ." My voice petered out

Why would I need to call anyone? Sure it was just the cerebellum that she couldn't find – by the next time I came back she would have found it. She had said it herself: it was probably the way that the baby was lying.

"Thanks, Mary, I'll call him later," I said.

Softly she wiped the cold slimy fluid from my stomach. She handed me the light-green piece of the paper, folded in two, and on it were the words *absent cerebellum*. She suggested that I talk to someone. She asked me if I was busy in the afternoon. I told her not really – that I didn't think so – so she said she would make an emergency afternoon appointment – a specialist consultant in that area would see me.

But I didn't know what the area of medicine for an absent cerebellum was.

"Afric, you will need to think about what you're going to call your baby, and you may need to decide soon. Would you like me to tell you if it's a girl or a boy?"

What was this woman on about? I had over three months to decide what to call the child – what was her hurry? It was a decision for Luke and me, one that we had intended to make together. Luke was particularly excited about choosing the name.

"Would this afternoon be okay, to hear, to find out?" I asked in a low voice, afraid I had answered incorrectly.

"Yes, this afternoon would be grand. It's just something that you might want to start thinking about." She smiled and helped me down from the table.

Then she turned off all the screens; she must have seen enough for a while.

She walked me out into the corridor.

"Go home – relax for a few hours – and then come back about four thirty – don't get too distressed. It will all be all right in the end." This time there was no encouraging smile.

I thanked her, nodded and got into the glass lift that would take me to the ground floor.

She was right – in the end it would be all right.

I got into Luke's big car. I'd always hated that car. Why did he need something so bloody big, for just the two of us? I turned the key in the ignition. I punched in **Coliemore Road** and a lady with a slight American twang told me it was twenty-two minutes to my destination.

"Afric," I said, "you need to keep it together for just twenty-two more minutes – concentrate." I hoped the sound of my own voice would soothe me. "Just keep the car on the left-hand side, inside the white line."

I switched on the radio very low, just so I was not alone.

The song sounded familiar. I knew it well but couldn't remember its title . . . what the hell was it? I had picked it up halfway through a verse. It sounded like Mick Jagger. Yes, I was pretty sure it was the Stones . . .

Suddenly a commercial break cut into the song and I clicked off the radio in disgust.

I looked down at my bloated belly. It spilled out over the seat belt like a man's oversized beer belly. Flesh peered out between the buttons of my shirt. I touched my stomach, just below the belly button; it was very firm and still.

I placed my hands in the ten-to-two position on the steering wheel, and I drove in the direction of home.

"Baby, you're going to have to tell me if you're sick. If you're sick your mum needs to know. How is your mum going to know what is wrong, unless you tell her? Is there something wrong, baby? I know that Mary thinks you're missing a cerebellum or something like that, but don't worry, baby. I'm sure it's not that important and that they'll find it anyway. They will, of course, find it and then you'll be okay – they just need to look harder for it. Do you know what I'm going to do? Do you know what I do when your dad loses stuff all the time? What I do is I pray to Saint Anthony. Saint Anthony is this fella – he lives up in the sky. Now for you to see him you need to look up, tilt your head up, stare out through my belly-button and up towards the sky, past the clouds and above the stars and into heaven. It's a different place from here – the people float around there all the time, cos they can't walk. Well, Saint Anthony, he lives there. And we're going to ask him to find that bloody cerebellum of yours cos Mary can't. Sure, can't he see everything from up there? That fella will find it, no bother! He doesn't need a scanner or any of that equipment – he just opens his eyes and he finds things."

She spoke again, the lady with the twang: '*Fifteen minutes to your destination.*'

"So, baby, you are not to listen to Mary. Don't worry, it will be fine. Of course we'll find it and then we'll just put it back where it's supposed to be at the back of your head."

I stopped at the traffic lights as they turned from red to flashing amber. I reached into my handbag and my fingertips touched the rough corners of the folded-over paper. Slowly I opened the paper, but the words were still there. '*Absent cerebellum*' it still said on the page. The words should have dissolved by now – they should have been eaten up by the paper. But they hadn't gone away because they were now our fate and they would never disappear. Those two new words I had just learnt were to become part of my new vocabulary.

I addressed my bump. "Mary is a silly silly woman not to find that thing at the back of your head. Do you know, baby, Mary needs to go to Specsavers – I'd say that she needs glasses. So the ad would start with a middle-aged lady, in a dark room, sitting down at a scanning machine. She is racing up and down a little baby's body, desperately looking for a baby's cerebellum, but she can't find it because she can't see it. Then she is transformed and the next day she comes into work, with very flashy purple glasses, and she scans the same baby, and then she finds the cerebellum, right there, where it should be at the back of the head. Wouldn't that be a brilliant ad for Specsavers? And the tagline would be: '*The future is safe with Specsavers.*' Yes, baby, she needs to go to Specsavers before we see her again. Isn't that a great idea for a commercial? I should call Specsavers and suggest that they use Mary for their next one."

I folded the green piece of paper that held my daughter's destiny and tucked it safely into my pink-and-cream handbag.

'*You have reached your destination,*' the lady chirped at me.

I'd been so busy chatting to the baby that I hadn't noticed that we were home.

I climbed up the grey granite steps; they felt steeper than usual. I opened the large bright-yellow door and went up the threadbare stairs to our apartment.

I poured myself a small chilled glass of white wine. I sat down at the desk in our bedroom that looks out at the white-and-grey lighthouse which is perched at the end of Howth's lush green headland.

Dublin Bay was still. There were no coloured boats on the water to cheer up the gloomy-looking sea.

Slowly, I opened my laptop, the red-and-black one. And onto the page I typed two words: **absent cerebellum**.

I looked from the screen to the lighthouse and then towards my phone. It read: **Luke calling**. I pushed the black rectangular button with the green line on it.

"Afric, Luke here."

I always wondered why he announced it was him at the end of the phone. Couldn't I see his name on the screen?

"Hi there, how are you doing?" I replied.

"Good, honey – more importantly, how are things with you two? How are you feeling?"

"Things are grand, absolutely grand," I lied. Well, in theory everything would be fine – in the afternoon.

"So tell me how the scan was? What could you see?" he continued enthusiastically.

There was a lag on his words so they were slightly delayed before they arrived to me.

"Okay, all seemed okay, but at this stage, at just over twenty-three weeks, it's hard to say. Well, they never know really until the baby is born, do they? But at a glance they seem to think everything is okay."

There was no need to tell him that there was something missing that they could not find. They would find it at four thirty, so there was no point in worrying him now. He was in China and there was nothing he could do. It wasn't like he could find it from there.

I clenched my hand and dug my nails hard into the palm. I sat upright on the black office chair. I focused on keeping my voice steady. I stared out to sea, directly ahead at twelve o'clock at the outline of the lighthouse. The sea was a charcoal grey; it had just started to rain. I focused on exchanging information, which was all I had to do: to provide him with the minimum necessary information with as little emotion as possible. I was just providing information, I told myself.

"How are you feeling though? Are you still tired in the evenings or is it better now? Is your back better?"

All these bloody questions, I thought. Why today couldn't we have one of the Yes-No conversations that we normally engaged in?

"It's better, thanks – those pains seemed to have stopped altogether," I replied. "So what is your news? Anything strange from your end?" Then, in an attempt to cut short the phone call, I continued: "Luke, Luke, it's really hard to hear you, the line isn't great!"

"Babes, I can hear you perfectly – it must be your side. Afric? Afric? I can hear you perfectly – do you want me to skype you instead?"

"No, no," I responded just a little too quickly. "I was just heading out the door for a swim before you called. It's been a long day and I'm hoping a dip will relax me."

"Okay, babes. Afric, don't overdo it with the swimming, especially when you have the precious cargo on board. It's good that all went well with the scan, isn't it? I'm starting to get really excited about us having a baby. It's great, isn't it?"

"Yes, Luke, it is, it is." I held the phone away from my mouth. I swallowed hard and looked out onto Dublin Bay. The lighthouse was only barely visible in the distance. Dark rainclouds obscured my vision.

"Afric, I am so sorry that I couldn't make it to this scan. I would have been there if I could have arranged it – just this time it wasn't possible. You understand, Afric, don't you? But I promise for sure that I'll be able to make all the rest of the appointments – in fact, you might send me the dates so I can put them in the diary."

I could tell by Luke's voice that he did regret not making it; his disappointment was genuine.

"Honestly, Luke, don't worry – most of the other

women there were on their own too – it's not a big deal at all, I promise." I was back on track now. I had managed to steady my voice – it was easier when he was doing most of the talking.

"My pregnancy app says that the kicking should start anytime soon, that it normally starts at twenty-two weeks. Have you felt anything, Afric?"

I didn't answer.

"Can you hear me, Afric?" he said and then repeated the question, at last registering that the phone coverage was not the best. "Can you hear me?"

"Yes – yes."

"Have you felt anything? The app says that it's like a sensation of having popcorn explode in your stomach – you should feel popping, just below the skin – have you felt anything like that, Afric ?"

I chuckled in an attempt to disguise my upset. "Really, Luke, you and your bloody app! You're hilarious, you really are!"

"Honestly, that's what it said – that from between week twenty and twenty-two you should be able to feel something, not quite kicking but an exploding-of-bubbles sensation. Afric, you know, I can't stop thinking about it. I am really excited – it's been a long time since I've been so excited about anything."

The clouds were bloated; they could no longer hold their moisture. The downpour hopped off the white horses; from where I sat it looked as though the rain was fighting with the sea.

"You know, when the baby is born I won't be

travelling so much – it will only be for the next few months . . ." He paused. "Afric, that I can promise. We will have time together before the baby is born to sort it all out. I know things have not been great between the two of us in the last few months, with me travelling and being away so much. It seems like you have a great routine going on and then when I come home I disrupt it. I get in the way and annoy you. I'm sorry, Afric, sorry if things haven't been easy in the last while."

I placed the handset between my ear and shoulder and squeezed both my fists this time, digging my nails deep into my palms, the white of my knuckles peering up at me.

"This time when I come back home, I promise I'll make more of an effort . . ." His voice trailed off.

"No, it's not all your fault – these bloody hormones make me impossible to live with. I am sorry too, really sorry, Luke." My voice began to tremble. I could feel my self-control slipping away from me. I pulled myself together and went on in an almost professional manner. "Let's leave it now and when you get back we can sort it out. We'll sit down and just work it out. I think that we just need to spend more time together as a family."

"Did they say if it was a boy or a girl?" he asked, ignoring my comments.

"They can see but I didn't ask," I replied, retaining the same professional tone.

"I am so sorry you had to go on your own, to the scan," he said.

I took advantage of the lag on the end of the phone to take a deep breath. "It was fine, really fine – it was only a scan," I lied.

"Afric, I'm so looking forward to coming home. I know this trip is very long one – more than a week away. I am really sorry – Afric, I miss you so much . . . I just want to be home." His tone was low, but not down.

"Love you, bye," was as much as I could manage. I was gone.

Chapter 3

So I got a taxi back there, to that building with the cream walls – same colour, just a different unit of the hospital. We whizzed past the seafront with people enjoying an early Friday-evening dip after a long day.

He had steel-grey hair, deep-blue eyes and a long white coat. The coat reached just below his knees; it flapped as though trying to keep up with him when he entered the room, a younger male understudy on his heels. He wore frameless glasses and he had some threatening-looking medical equipment dangling from his neck like an oversized necklace. He had a kind face. My mother always told me that you get the face you deserve in life. It was the type of face that you feel you could talk to, openly. My first impression was that he definitely deserved his caring face.

He told me it was a pleasure to meet me. I

thanked him – I thought the pleasure must be all his. I would never consider an appointment with a foetal abnormalities obstetrician as enjoyment.

"Afric, did you come in on your own this afternoon?" he asked.

"Yes, my husband is away on business at the moment – he works abroad. He's in China until next Friday – he would be here otherwise." I felt it only fair that I should defend Luke in his absence.

He seemed to consider my response as reasonable, but not ideal.

His silence encouraged me to try to fill the gap.

"It's Luke's busy time of the year, so he's away a lot pretty much from April through until July. I'm used to it now – well, it's like anything – I suppose you get used to it, don't you? It's like being single all over again but with the security of being married, if you know what I mean."

"Really?" was all he said.

"Well, yes," I replied lamely.

"Did you tell anyone that you had an appointment here today?" he asked clinically.

"Yes, I told my mum, Lizzy. I told her there might be something wrong."

He seemed a bit more impressed with that response. He looked anxious, as though he was done with the formalities and now it was time to get down to business.

"You hop up there." Gently he indicated for me to move towards the examination table. "Let me have a look at your baby."

I lay back and rolled up my top so that my bump was looking up at him.

"You know the procedure by now, don't you?" he said.

"I do," I replied.

"I believe Mary scanned you this morning and there were a few things she was concerned about?"

"Yes. She said there seemed to be some things that were not quite correct – she never got to the end of her list – there were things that she couldn't find?" I surprised myself with how confidently I spoke about something I knew very little about.

"Afric, what do you understand from that?" he asked in a schoolteacher manner.

"Well, as of earlier today, I have a new vocabulary: three new words." I sounded like a school kid answering the teacher. I steadied my voice and fixed my gaze on the calendar directly ahead of me. I didn't look at him, his understudy or the nurse who had just entered the room. "I understand that there may be a question of the baby having an absent cerebellum, or a deformed cerebellum. Mary also spoke of possible talipes in the left foot." My eyes remained fixed on the calendar.

He seemed satisfied with this response. "Well, let me have a look at what I can see and we can take it from there," he said.

"Okay, that's fine," I replied, trying not to show I was scared.

His deep-blue eyes looked at me straight. "Yes," he said. "It will all be okay in the end." He said it in such a way that it sounded like hospital code for something else.

The female nurse sported equally dangerous-looking artillery; it just hung there from her thin neck. Without uttering a word, she leaned in beside the man with the blue eyes and squirted gunge on my ruinous bump. She never did use the dangling gadget or utter a single word.

The cold fierce-looking steel hand-piece of the monitor dug into my stomach.

"If I don't talk it's not that there is something wrong," he said. "Where I can I will talk you through what is happening."

His understudy remained silent.

"Your baby," he announced out of the blue, "is a girl."

Just like that. All my dreams of guessing and wondering were gone. It was a girl. I didn't reply.

My tiny baby girl was once again on a giant wall-monitor in black-and-white. Three sets of eyes were fixed on her every move on the smaller screen. He concentrated his efforts on her tiny head. To the naked eye, her head seemed a few sizes too small for her dainty body. He tilted his own head at different angles as he examined the screen.

"Your baby has a very strong heartbeat," he said.

It was that bloody heart that continued to pump blood at a fierce rate around her underdeveloped body and kept her alive.

"Okay, I have seen what I need to see," he said to his understudy, who remained nameless and silent but took it as his cue to leave the room.

The efficient nurse gently wiped all the gel gunge from my stomach. Then she was gone too.

"Afric, you can sit up whenever you're ready." He offered me his arm in the same way that a wrestler invites his opponent to an arm-wrestle.

I sat up with his help and swung my legs over the side of the examination table. He sat down facing me.

"I can confirm that what Mary told you is correct," he said in a low clear voice. "There is an absent cerebellum and possible talipes and there may even be other complications that we can't know about at this early stage. Afric . . ." He looked straight at me, right in the eyes, and his deep-blue eyes looked as though they might pierce my heart. "Afric, if your baby makes it to full term she will be both mentally and physically handicapped – that's if she does make it to full term. And if she does, she may survive only days, or maybe only hours after she is born – at most a few months – she won't survive for very long. At this stage, I cannot say exactly how severely physically or mentally handicapped she will be, but from what I have seen today, your baby will be profoundly handicapped."

Then he said those dread words.

"I am afraid your baby is incompatible with life. Incompatible with life, Afric." He repeated it as though to confirm what he had said. "Your baby has a foetal abnormality that is fatal." He paused. "There are a few different syndromes where the cerebellum is either partially or fully absent. At a crude first glance from the scans it would appear that your little girl has an absent cerebellum. We can see no evidence of a cerebellum at all. This we can tell by the measurements we have taken of the baby's head circumference."

I swallowed hard. My concentration was fierce. I did not want to miss a single word. I needed to take it all in, to remember all these new phrases, so that I understood it all . . . so I could comprehend how sick my little girl was.

He continued with his clear and coherent diagnosis. "Some of the syndromes associated with an absent or partially absent cerebellum are Edwards Syndrome, Dandy-Walker Syndrome, Patau Syndrome and Joubert Syndrome. Some are fatal – others are not. An absent cerebellum is strong evidence of a serious condition where there is very limited brain development, other deformities such as problems with the spine, and with the feet – in your baby's case it seems that is so – we can see evidence of talipes. An absent cerebellum can be an indicator of Patau Syndrome – but it could be, as I said, any one of a range of syndromes. Afric, we cannot at this stage tell you which syndrome it is. We would need to perform an amniocentesis in order to establish which one your baby has."

He waited for me to respond, but I had no words to give him, so I nodded, a gentle nod.

"The syndromes are a result of a problem with chromosomes. You see, each person has twenty-three pairs of chromosomes, or forty-six in all, in each cell. For each pair of chromosomes you get one from your mother and one from your father. Any changes in the number of chromosomes, whether too many or too few, can result in disorders. In other cases there may be a change in the structure of chromosomes – some of the structure might be missing, repeated or altered – this too can cause these syndromes or disorders.

"An amniocentesis will give us a clearer picture of what was wrong with your baby's chromosomes – it will also tell us if the problem is genetic or not." The man with the deep-blue eyes addressed my eyes. "I would recommend that you have that now, here. I can perform it immediately for you."

"Amniocentesis . . ." My mind wandered. I had heard so many different terms, so many unfamiliar terms, that my brain was frazzled. I must have seemed puzzled as I looked into his eyes. They were now more of a grey than a blue colour.

"What it means is we take a sample of amniotic fluid, using a hollow needle, from the uterus. An amniocentesis will detect ninety-nine per cent of chromosomal disorders. If we request the results of the test as a matter of urgency from Scotland we can get them back first thing on Monday morning. And we will then be clear as to what condition exactly your baby has. But, Afric – the results will not change the fact that your baby is incompatible with life. It might be a good idea to familiarise yourself with these syndromes, the ones I mentioned. The nurse will give you a list of them – best now to understand what you're facing."

I smiled half a smile, just to acknowledge what he had said.

"I'm afraid, Afric, there is very little else we can do for you." He pursed his lips and very gently shook his head. He seemed genuinely sorry he couldn't help any further. "There are decisions that you – you two as a couple need to make – together – to decide how to deal with this incompatibility."

I sat there, upright on the examination table, like a lost little girl. It was like someone had flicked a switch in my life and my world turned from colour to a dull black-and-white. Along with the colour, my hopes, dreams and wishes for the future evaporated into thin air in the room with cream walls.

His steel-blue eyes awaited my reaction.

I had no words, nothing to say, so I thanked him. Imagine thanking someone for telling you that your baby was incompatible with life. Surely he must have thought that a little odd?

I was relieved this time he didn't tell me it was a pleasure. How could it be a pleasure for him to have to tell a mother such a horrible reality?

That was why they gave him the kind face. That face had seen a lot of hurt.

Chapter 4

A Saturday in June, 2013

"NHS Royal Merseyside Women's Hospital. How may I direct your call?"

I opened my mouth to speak but the words would not come out – they had got stuck, lost somewhere between the back of my throat and my lips.

"Hello? Hello – NHS Royal Merseyside Women's Hospital – how may I direct your call?"

I hung up.

I walked from the bedroom through to the living room, and back to the bedroom. I sat back down at the window with the view of the sea and redialled the same number. This time I told the very efficient lady with the cockney accent that I needed the Foetal Medicine Unit.

"Yes, my dear, I will connect you just now."

I waited.

"The line is busy – can you hold for a moment?" she enquired efficiently.

"Okay."

Some elevator music played in the background; mindlessly I hummed to the familiar tune.

A different accent enquired gently if I wanted a consultation.

"Yes, please."

"Let me see. Yes, you're in luck – there's been a cancellation. We can fit you in this Monday." She sounded delighted with this.

I wasn't. "Monday . . . Monday . . . do you not have anything sooner than that? Is there any chance you could fit me in tomorrow, please? I can come straight away – I can get a flight today and be with you tomorrow morning – first thing in the morning?"

"Today is Saturday," she said curtly, "and we don't do consultations in the NHS on a Sunday unless they are emergencies."

"Yes, sorry, that will be fine – please book me in for Monday – that is this Monday coming, isn't it? Sorry, I just want to be sure?"

"Yes, Monday – the day after tomorrow."

"But if you get a cancellation later today, maybe you could slot me in sooner?"

She ignored my last comment. "If you can make it here by ten in the morning we will see you then." This was followed by a "Please hold".

I could tell by her tone that this was the end of the conversation.

It felt all wrong. As if she didn't understand how serious my problem was. God, maybe I had in error called a clinic in Liverpool where they did plastic surgery, face-lifts and that kind of thing? *Jesus*, I thought, maybe I had just booked myself in for a face-lift unknowingly. It was not that I didn't need one – I did and never more so than in the last few days – the lines on my forehead were now ridges – but at the moment I had more urgent matters to attend to.

The hold music chirped in the background. It was the Rolling Stones, I was sure of it this time. "Beast of Burden" was the tune. She was still gone. I was still holding. And they were still singing.

I must have dialled the wrong number. Sure they hadn't even asked me what I needed done or who I needed to see. Definitely I had called a plastic-surgery clinic by mistake – that was why they never had cancellations – sure why would someone who had been considering a face-lift for years, not to mind having saved up for it, then suddenly decide to cancel it at the last minute?

"Yes, where were we?" She was back in an even more efficient voice. "Yes – Monday at ten it is."

I thought about asking her about the face-lift, but she seemed very busy so I decided against it.

"May I have your personal details?" she enquired.

Now that we had agreed a date and a time on her terms and conditions, the frosty manner seemed to have thawed somewhat.

"Afric Lynch," I replied.

"You sound Irish – are you a resident of the UK?" she asked.

"No, no, I am not – is that okay?" I enquired nervously, afraid that I might piss her off again.

"Of course it is, no problem at all. We have an Irish package – that is the only reason I asked, darling. If you give me your email address we will send you the details."

Oh Jesus, this is definitely a bloody plastic-surgery clinic – sure why else would they be offering an Irish package? I had read about them before in women's magazines that I read at the hairdresser's and they advertised them at the back of the English Sunday newspapers, with before and after photos. They advertised themselves as: **A Whole New You** – *all-inclusive Irish package with flights, face, three nights' accommodation, meals and refreshments included.*

"And how many weeks pregnant are you, darling?" she enquired.

"I'll be twenty-four weeks on Monday," I answered, almost relieved.

She efficiently worked through other queries and then asked me if I'd had an amniocentesis.

"Yes, I had," I replied.

"Good, that will make things easier. Now, Afric – I will need you to sign a little consent form allowing us to request your results from the lab in Scotland – we do this quite often – contact them directly once we have your consent – it means when the consultant sees you on Monday he or she will have all the information they need to make an informed decision – is that okay?"

I said yes – because I could not think of anything more to say.

"The consultant will see you and then we can take it from there. Do you have any questions?" Now her tone was even softer.

"No, I don't at the moment, I don't think so." Was I meant to, I wondered.

"Okay, so we look forward to meeting you on Monday morning at ten. Afric, a lot of our Irish clients prefer to check in on the Sunday afternoon or evening – there's an early afternoon flight from Dublin, or a later evening one. We can arrange to have a bed here for you on Sunday night. It might be easier for you – then you won't be rushed on Monday morning, or concerned about finding the hospital."

"I haven't even looked at flights but, yes, I think that would be best. I'll try to book that early afternoon flight."

"Just let me know and I'll arrange to have a bed available for you on Sunday evening. My name is Jane, by the way – when you get to reception, ask for Jane. I won't be here tomorrow evening but I'll be here on Monday morning first thing and I'll look after you myself. Just bring yourself – we will look after everything else."

"Thank you, see you Monday, Jane," I managed to utter.

I hung up and set about booking the flight. That done, I phoned Liverpool to let Jane know.

Then I sat down at the window. The sea and the

sky were a grey-blue; I could barely see the silhouette of the white-and-grey lighthouse perched on the edge of the headland today. It looked vulnerable, like it might fall off the cliff and into the sea. The gorse's brilliant yellow seemed now more of a softer primrose colour. Odd, I thought, for a Saturday, that there were no coloured sails drifting past the eaves of the house at the end of the street. I looked at the ruby-coloured cherry tree below my window – its leaves were motionless – that was why the boats weren't in the bay.

I turned on the radio for company, the one by my bedside locker. I had my little girl but I needed some adult company, or maybe it was a distraction that I required.

"*We are celebrating a weekend of the Rolling Stones – yes, it's a Rolling Stones love-in for the next forty-eight hours – listen every hour on the hour for a Rolling Stones classic – stay right here on Easy FM with Alison Dempsey all weekend for the best from the Stones! And now for one of the all-time Stones' greats – do you recognise this?*"

It was the same song I had heard in the car and this time I recognised it: "Goodbye, Ruby Tuesday."

I sat at the window and looked through the fingerprints that stained the inside of it. They made the sea look smudged and they obscured the outline of the lighthouse. A few sails now appeared just above the jagged slate eaves of the house at the end of the street – they were not inside the left-handed fingerprints so they were brighter, much brighter.

The cherry tree moved ever so slightly in the early-afternoon summer breeze. Luke was right – it was more of a ruby than a cherry colour.

I rubbed my little girl very gently in a soothing circular movement. I was tired after the shocking morning. I lay on the bed, with the window ajar, and I hummed the Stones' song about the girl they were going to miss . . .

I drifted off to sleep, my hand on my doomed belly, my little girl's gentle movements lulling me to sleep.

I woke up startled, not sure what time it was. The clock on the bedside radio announced it was 15.44. I needed to get organised for my outing to Liverpool. We needed to pack – we had a lot of things to do before leaving tomorrow.

Also I would need to talk to Luke.

Our little girl would need an outfit . . . and of course a name.

I walked down the threadbare stairs, out the yellow door and onto the street. I headed in the direction of the shops. When I walked I didn't feel that my feet were touching the ground.

"Hi there, can I help you? Is it boys' or girls' things that you're looking for? Do you want to tell me the age of the baby?" the over-eager sales assistant enquired.

I just looked blankly at her and remained motionless and speechless.

Then word for word she repeated her questions,

this time a little bit slower – perhaps she thought that I didn't speak English as a first language.

I smiled at her in acknowledgement of her presence and then walked to the back of the shop to escape her intrusive enquiries.

There, safely tucked away, I tried to figure out the answer. I thought I should say six months, because I was six months pregnant – was that correct? However, if it was a newborn baby, then it was the newborn clothes I needed to look at. The baby would be newborn but three months premature so maybe they had a premature section that operated in minus figures. I wandered around through aisles and rows of pretty colourful outfits. There were three to six months sizes but I needed minus six to minus three months.

Should I ask the over-efficient sales lady? No, that was drawing too much attention to my situation. I settled on describing my baby as newborn. Technically that was correct, and anyway she would be a newborn baby to me.

The sales assistant had sneaked down to the back of the shop and now stood only a few metres from me. I was cornered, trapped between her and a row of tiny babygros.

"It's difficult to choose an outfit for a baby when you aren't sure what they look like or even what sex they are, isn't it?" she said.

Difficult to choose, assuming that the child is going to be normal, I thought. Even more difficult when you're choosing an outfit for a baby whose deformities you are unsure of. Should I get two babygros in different sizes just in case she was more distorted than I hoped?

"Indeed," I replied. I dug my nails into the palm of my hand and stared past her, then turned away. I squeezed my eyes shut, very hard, to stop the tears. I could feel my eyelids beginning to tremble; the tears were not far off pouring down my face.

Black would be an appropriate colour for her outfit, I thought. All the clothes were bright, happy, vibrant colours. There were no dull browns or blacks in this baby shop. Probably because having a baby is meant to be a joyous occasion. Nor was there a section for premature stillborn babies.

I selected a single blue outfit, for the saddest day of my life. Eighteen months previously I had selected a simple oyster-coloured outfit for the happiest day. The light-blue babygro had a picture of a cuddly elephant on the left-hand side. The elephant was a deeper blue – it made him look bigger. White buttons ran down the front. Also, dangling from the small padded hanger was a little hat. I looked at the baby outfit and down at my ruinous bump.

"Would that fit you? Would you like the colour blue for your big day?" I whispered to my baby. I looked out of the left-hand corner of my eye to see if the nosy assistant had heard me talking to my little girl but she had gone back to the cash register.

I went to pay.

"Is that for yourself?" She made it sound like I might be wearing it. "Aren't you great to be getting organised so early – that's what I always say to mums-to-be – get the shopping done early in case you go early." The words were trotted out like she must have used this line thousands of time.

I just looked at her, expressionless, wishing the blue babygro was for someone else and not my fatally ill child.

She looked at my face, down at my bump, back at my eyes and then fixed her eyes on the task of folding the tiny blue piece of cloth.

"I see," she said. She swiped my credit card, popped the baby-blue outfit in a brown-paper bag, folded it over, handed me a receipt. The once overeager assistant was now silent. "Good luck," she said, but this time she didn't look at me but beyond me.

That song popped into my head again – "Ruby Tuesday". It just stuck there, refusing to move. I walked slowly up the street, humming it.

I pushed open the large yellow door and walked up the shabby stairs. I sat at the window, looking out on to Dublin bay. The sea was a steel grey. I could not see the lighthouse, and the outline of the headland across the bay was only barely visible. There were triangles of white on the sea; there was a yacht race on, the sails gliding across the white horses.

I poured myself a glass of white wine. There was no fear now that a few glasses of wine would damage our tiny baby's brain development. God, I thought, we had got it so wrong,

My little girl began to kick and kick. I paced the room to settle her. I walked to the white wardrobe and then back to the window. Was she kicking me to remind me that she was there? So that when she was gone I would remember how it felt to have her inside me? Was she kicking me for her final thirty-six hours to torture me? Revenge for making her such a sick child, for making her imperfect in every way? Kicking me so that I could never forget carrying her? Or maybe she was saying a long goodbye, and this was part of her exit strategy.

I hoped that the wine might make her a little tipsy and she would nod off to sleep. She was in full flight now, kicking like hell. Mary was right; my baby had very long femurs and a powerful heart.

I drank, she kicked, she kicked and I drank. It was as if we were having our one and only mother-daughter battle. I cried and the kicking eased, the gentle motion of my sobs and the wine lulling her to sleep.

I lay the tiny clothes on our king-sized bed. They looked so minute there. They were lost lying there. I opened my red-and-black laptop. There in my Gmail account was a list of things that I needed to consider before tomorrow or latest Monday morning.

First, though, my tiny girl needed a name.

I had to give our baby a name that I had chosen for her, not one that *we* had chosen. There would not be any long discussions about names. No poring over top-ten lists of old or new Irish names. I wondered if it would be easier to name a baby that was going to survive. Yes, trying to name a baby that is going to die was more difficult. You don't want to call the baby after anyone; well, no one is going to appreciate you naming your dead baby after them, are they? I wouldn't be very impressed if someone named their deceased baby after me. To name a living baby after a person would be okay – but a dead one, no thanks.

I should try to find a name that had no connection or association to anybody, or to any place, a name that was free of connection. It needed to be free of emotions too. Whatever name I chose would be my tiny girl's name forever, so it must not be chosen in an overemotional state. Also, if you know that the baby is not going to live you don't want to use your favourite name, in case sometime in the future you may have a healthy living child. Her healthy sibling might not want to be named after her dead deformed sister.

I stared blankly out at the sea; I had about thirty-six hours to name our child.

Chapter 5

"Hello, darling, how are you feeling?" Luke sounded very upbeat.

"Grand, just a bit tired. I get lazy by the end of the day." I concentrated my gaze on Howth Head. The sea was a dark charcoal colour, the lights of Howth separating the dark land from the grey sea. "How are things with you?"

"Fine, nothing too eventful – worked, swam, ate, slept – the same routine as always when I am away on business, nothing new," he replied.

Thankfully, we were veering towards one of those Yes-No conversations. I was hoping it would be more of a formality than a full-scale chat, because I had to concentrate on the important thing: telling him about the trip to Liverpool.

"And what did you do today – anything exciting? Did you swim?" He appeared to be just going through the motions with the conversation.

"What did I do today?" I repeated back his question to him. "I got up this morning, didn't do much, went for a stroll and then did a bit of shopping."

"Oh great – did you buy anything nice?" he enquired, obviously trying to prolong the conversation.

I looked at the tiny blue babygro on the bed. "No, nothing nice, I just strolled around the shops," I lied casually – I was getting better at it, the lying. "Luke, listen, I just had a call from work and the IT manager was due to go to a conference in Liverpool for two days, Monday and Tuesday, but he has come down with some type of a bug so he can't make it – so they called me this morning and asked me could I go instead? Well, they didn't really ask me, they told me, so I'm flying out late tomorrow night and I'll be back late on Wednesday." I paused, waiting for his reaction. I was also surprised how my lies designed for Luke rolled so easily off my tongue.

"Well, this is a bit much, isn't it?" he responded, sounding annoyed.

"It is, I guess, but given that I'm always telling them they need to move into this century IT-wise, I couldn't then say no when they had bothered to invest in the conference."

"True," he replied. "True. Where are you staying? Where is the conference?"

I hesitated. I glared at the sea, hoping my prepared answer would pass his scrutiny.

"Afric, can you hear me? Where did they say the conference was?"

"They didn't say – somewhere in Liverpool – no doubt in some terrible conference hotel. They just wanted to check I would attend first. They said that they'd send me on all the details but nothing has come through yet." I exhaled, almost proud of my subterfuge.

"Grand – just let me know where you're staying – just for emergencies."

"Sure."

Then I told him I loved him and said goodbye.

"Are you sure everything is okay, Afric? You don't seem yourself . . . you don't seem to be in the best of form . . ."

"Yes, yes, honestly, I'm fine – it's just these bloody hormones are driving me crazy – highs and low, that's all it is. And now a trip to Liverpool that I really need like a hole in my head." I was just about holding it together.

"Any sign of the baby kicking yet?"

"I knew that there was something I was going to say to you! How could I have forgotten? Yes, in the last day or so, the baby has started kicking. And, Luke, do you know what? I think it's a girl, that our baby is a little girl." I paused, waiting for a reaction.

"You think it's a girl – why do you say that?"

"Just something, I don't know what it is, tells me it's a girl." I held my breath. I didn't want to hear any trace of disappointment from him. Not now.

"Afric, no point in guessing at this stage." His response was efficient and matter of fact.

"You're right, of course. I'm off for a swim now.

Talk to you tomorrow, love you, bye."

"Take care, Afric."

"I will."

I hung up.

I opened the white wardrobe and carefully selected a long grey nightdress. Grey seemed to be the most appropriate colour. My bright pink dressing gown would be too happy, too vibrant for such a sad occasion, so I left it behind. I placed my slippers, socks, underwear and shoes in my blue hold-all. I scanned the wardrobe for some clothes that I did not hold any emotional attachment to – items that I was sure I would not ever wear again. I selected a moss top and a pair of faded black jeans with an elasticated waist. I folded them neatly and put them inside the case.

I placed the tiny blue newborn baby outfit and my camera into the bag. I put in a picture of our wedding day. In the picture all our family and friends are with us in the garden. You can see a tree. I wanted to show her that tree, the tree in the front garden where I used to play we were young. In the picture it is only barely visible but I could tell her about it. There were a lot of people in that photo – would I have enough time with her to tell her about them all? I mean, if I was going to tell her about all one hundred and fifty people both she and I would be exhausted.

The picture was taken on the 21st June 2011. We wanted the bash for our friends and family to be a memorable party and to go on as long as possible, so we chose the longest day of the year. At the wedding the sun didn't set until ten o'clock and then we danced the night away with all our family and friends. We partied and drank till dawn. Afterwards, we were satisfied that we made the best possible use of every minute of the longest day of the year.

I would need to decide who I would tell her about in the picture. I looked up from the desk and back out to sea. I would need to make a list – if I forgot someone important in that picture and she had never been introduced to them, then in years to come when I'd meet them again I might feel guilty. A list would be best, I concluded.

I completed the list. I got it down to twenty-two people. That seemed a pretty good compromise, down from one hundred and fifty, I thought. Then, I rechecked it, added names, deleted names, added more names, and deleted others.

How would I start the conversation with her, with my little girl? Would I say 'How are you?' Obviously not too good because she'd be dead. Or 'What do you want to do today?' There would be no answer, so then I would show her the photo, and point to each of the people in it, spending two or three minutes on each person. They would be funny stories; I would entertain her with the photo.

Tomorrow, I would take my little girl on a whirlwind tour of my life, to a few places that were very special to me in Dublin. If I took her to those places, I would have already covered an introduction to a lot of my family and friends and then our schedule on Monday would not be so tight. Then, when she and I were together, I would tell her about her dad, her grandparents, her aunts and uncles. I would tick them off the list just in case I forgot anyone.

My tiny angel still needed a name, or at least as a minimum a working title, like you would give a book a temporary name. 'Angel' I liked because she was my angel. I pronounced it as they do in Spain, in my best Spanish accent: "*Ang-hel, Ang-hel.*" It seemed to fit her, to suit her; soon she would be my angel and later our angel. Angel would be her name for now until I found the perfect name to call my little girl, a special name for her alone.

Chapter 6

A Sunday in June, 2013

My alarm went off early that Sunday morning. It was just after seven. I had been awake since five, thinking about the day ahead. It both terrified and excited me. I had breakfast at the window, strong black coffee and a cinnamon bagel with cream cheese. The coffee tasted bitter and the bagel was like cardboard. I drank less coffee than normal; I wanted to be calm for our big outing. Also I wanted to avoid toilet stops – the fewer humans I encountered today the better.

It was a beautiful summer's day; we had a magnificent day for our outing. It was the type of a day when you know why you love living by the sea.

"The only problem with these days, my little angel, is the mass exposure of Irish flesh. The sunshine brings out people who have a tangerine look. The colour is like some rare form of jaundice. When your dad first came to live here, it was a fantastic summer and he said to me: 'Afric, why do so many women here in Ireland have an orange-ish colour? Why are they the colour of Fanta?' I looked at him. 'What you are talking about, Luke – how do you mean "orange"?' I asked. 'Their skin is orange,' he replied. I had to explain that it was fake tan. You see, where your dad comes from it's so hot that they don't need fake tan, so he had never seen it before. So since that day your dad and I call them the Fanta People and we count the number of orange people that we see on a sunny day. So, Angel, will you and I do that? Count the Fanta People today? The sun is out so they will be too."

Dublin Bay was a deep cobalt blue. There was no one on the water, only the usual grey-and-black buoys that day-trippers confuse with seals. I could see Howth Lighthouse across the bay; there it stood majestically on the end of its headland. The yellow gorse stood out in contrast to the green and sandstone-coloured sea cliffs that peered down into the Irish Sea.

A beautiful morning for a journey, I thought. My little girl will see my life in full sunshine. I double-checked my itinerary: I had the entire morning to give my daughter a guided tour of my life in Dublin. I hoped that she would enjoy it. Though it would be one of the saddest days of my life, and my heart would ache, I didn't want my sorrow to colour the stories. My life up to now had been very privileged.

I printed out the list of destinations and of characters that I didn't want to forget to tell Angel about. I put the list together with the green piece of paper that Mary had given me and I put the photo with them too. All the important paperwork was now together.

The plan was to visit six places in all, starting at about eight o clock; we were going to get going early before the Sunday drivers invaded the seaside roads.

I wore a black T-shirt that just about covered my bump, black trousers with an elasticated waistband, a bright pink cotton scarf and pink Converse boots. The pink, I thought, would cheer up the black.

"Now, my angel, we are going to head off on our adventure, just you and me." I rubbed my stomach in a circular direction. "Say goodbye to the apartment – wave bye-bye – we won't be coming back here again."

I picked up my hand luggage, and walked slowly down the steps with their frayed carpet. I pulled the large yellow door shut firmly behind me. She kicked me softly; maybe she was telling me that she was looking forward to the outing. The display on my phone read: 08:03.

"Let's go, darling." There was no response. "At least there won't be any traffic at this time of the morning." I bleeped open the car. "Right, darling, we're off! Our first stop on the whirlwind tour today is just down the street – in fact we could have probably walked down to the village, to the main street – well, anyway – look there, that is where she lived. Penny, that was her pet name. Penny is the lady who will look after you when you have to go from me – so it would be good if you knew a little more about her – so that when you go to her you will be able to tell her you saw her house – well, it is more of a home than a house. Penny told the best stories but sometimes you couldn't understand what she was saying, she was laughing so much. I will always remember the sound of her laughing – it was infectious. She had long flowing dresses in different vibrant colours; she had a deep cerise one that she wore for very special occasions. She had a green one too – it was like the colour of grass in the middle of summer – it was a lush green. Another was a deep blue like the colour of Dublin Bay on a clear summer's day, a kind of electric blue. They were all the same style, simple and elegant. She had lots of brooches, with coloured stones, and she always wore them on the left-hand side of her dress.

"Penny lived there, see, in that small house with the black door. See, Angel, just there next door to the pub. She used to say that one day they were going to drill a hole in the wall like a hatch, so that they could put their hand through it and a gin and tonic would magically be placed in their hands. They never did drill that hole in the wall.

"Behind that door is a home full of treasures. When I say 'treasures' I don't mean expensive ones but ones that tell of a full and happy life. That house is stuffed with the happiest memories. Paintings that people have done of the two of them gazing into each other's eyes – they were so in love, until the day she died. He is still so in love with her. You know, Angel, your dad and I were like that when we first married. Sometimes in life you get distracted and forget what is really important. They never got sidetracked – they always knew what was important: each other and other people were all that was important in the world. They have all sorts of photos – black-and-white – some in focus, some very out of focus – photos of famous and not so famous people, but mostly photos of just ordinary people. They would throw loads of parties for their friends; she would say you can never have too many parties. When we were younger they would give us jobs helping at their lunches. There were always lots of people. We would spill red wine on their beautiful outfits and we dropped twice as much food as we ever managed to serve. She would introduce us as her helpers for the day. After we had messed up people's beautiful clothes and they had left hungry because most of it was on the floor, she would hand us wads of notes and tell us what a great help we were.

"So that's Penny's house. You will remember that, won't you, the one with the black door? Right, let's go . . ."

We drove along the sea front and on towards Bullock Harbour. The blue-and-white fishing boats were lined up in the water, waiting eagerly for people to rent them. They looked lonely bobbing around there. Each boat had a different name – most were girls' names, painted in white against a cornflower-blue background on the outside of the boat, on the stern.

I pulled the car up closer – so we could see the names more clearly.

"Let's have a look and see if there's a boat with your nickname on it – maybe there's an 'Angel' there, or maybe there will be a name on a boat that might suit you. If we saw a name there that we liked, it wouldn't mean that you were called after a boat – it would just be that we got our inspiration from a boat . . ."

We found a Maria, a Patsy, an Aoife, a John Abo and others, but no Angel. They probably had an Angel boat and it was just that a keen fisherman had rented it for his early-morning fishing trip. I told her it was out in the bay.

"Oh God, Angel, look at the time! Your mum is rambling on again – I hope that I'm not boring you to death. I'm not sticking to the schedule – come on, let's go!"

I stopped the car just beyond Joyce's Tower in Sandycove. I decided against telling her about Joyce, because I had far more important people to tell her about, and anyway he wasn't in the photograph with the tree.

We got out and walked down to the steps of the 'The Forty Foot'. We were alone except for a few early-morning swimmers.

"Angel, you've been swimming here lots of times. See that harbour over there to the right? That is Bullock Harbour, where we just came from, just now – it's where your dad and I often swim to. It's beautiful here, isn't it? So calm. You have swum to the harbour lots and lots of time – not bad for a minus-three-month old.

"Your dad wants to live there by the harbour. He says when we win the Lotto we will buy one of those houses, the tall houses – can you see them? That one there, the house that has the sea as its back garden. He says then he would get up every morning very early and go fishing. You know, Angel, I thought he was going to be just a tiny bit disappointed when we discovered you were a 'she' and not a 'he'. I was quite nervous about telling him – he had said once he would like to have a little boy he could teach to fish – but I needed him to know because, well, if he was disappointed better to get it out of the way early on. So I asked him if he was disappointed about the fishing. But do you know what he said to me, Angel? He said: 'I would love to teach my little girl to fish.'" It was only a small white lie that I had told my little girl. "I was so happy because I didn't want him to be sad, to get that terrible deep sadness. I hope that he doesn't get too sad when you are gone." I rubbed my stomach in a circular motion. "He will miss you very much, Angel.

"See there, the other side of the steps? That's where we'd swim towards Dun Laoghaire Harbour. That was one of our favourite swims. You and I often swam it – that was where we would swim when your dad was away. You and I, we would swim out to the yellow buoys – see the buoys over there? When you are out there in the middle of the sea, when you breathe to the left, you can see all of Dun Laoghaire with its church spires. Then when you turn around, on the way back, breathing to the left gives you views of Howth Head with its patches of different colour greens and sometimes yellow. When we were together in the water I would talk to you – were you able to hear me then, my little girl? Or were you always sick? My favourite time of the year to swim is when the bright yellow gorse is there.

"You know, sometimes the water is so cold here that your head feels like ice when you get in. I often wondered if you could ever feel the cold when I dived in." I paused and waited as though I was expecting her to answer. "Angel, how stupid of me – of course you couldn't feel the cold. How silly of me! You would never have felt cold with your absent cerebellum. I am relieved to know that you were never cold out there in the big blue sea.

"Look, Angel, the swimmers are swimming around the yellow buoys – that's our swim. Your dad and I often wondered if you were going to like to swim like we both did. We had decided early on that we were not going to be parents who forced their kids to do things that *we* liked. But your dad read somewhere online – or maybe it was the bloody pregnancy apps that he reads at me – and anyway it said that if you do lots of outdoor activities while you are pregnant the baby will get used to the motion, sleep better, and then will love the great outdoors. God, after reading that, any time he was home, which was not too often thankfully in that respect, he had me worn out from all the activities:

swimming, fishing, kayaking and hiking.

"We had better go. I am chattering on and those swimmers are on their way back in here. We wouldn't want them to think I'm nuts, talking to you, would we?"

I sat into the driver's seat and wrapped the seatbelt around my little girl to keep her safe.

As we motored on down the sea road, heading for Dun Laoghaire, the morning traffic both human and vehicular was picking up, hardly surprising on such a beautiful summer's morning.

"Do you see there on the left-hand side, the park just there with the big playground? Do you see it, just there? That is where your dad and I used to go every Sunday. People often go to church as a ritual on a Sunday but we would go for a sea swim to the Forty Foot, and then we would stop off here at the Farmers' Market.

"Back then we would hold hands. Your dad's left hand would hold my right hand, but not the whole hand – only the first three fingers of my hand. The last two were never included – he would leave them just dangling there excluded from the intimacy. I could never understand that. I would say 'Luke, what about the other fingers – they feel left out!' and he would shrug and say, 'It's more comfortable this way.' I would give him a half smile just so he would know that I did not approve of his favouritism. Your dad likes things a certain way – he likes when things stay the same – it makes him feel more safe like that.

"Our first stop every Sunday in the market would

be at the cheesemonger. Your dad, he loves cheese, particularly blue cheeses. 'Can I have your best big ripe Irish blue cheese?' he would ask the Catalan cheesemonger, Fabiana. He could never remember any of the cheeses' names. He would take half of one brand name and the end of another and stick them together, so that the names he asked for were always jumbled up, causing complete confusion at the busy cheese stand. Fabiana always seemed to think it amusing, even if she was under more pressure communicating with him, rather than selling cheese to impatient customers.

"I think that Fabiana always liked to see him coming in through the elegant silver gates of the park to the Farmers' Market. He told me one time that she thought he was an Australian or New Zealand rugby player – I think he was kind of chuffed, but of course he would never say that. He liked the fact that she was a foreigner too – it was like their own 'in joke'. I would leave them to it and wander off to the book stand.

"Do you know, Fabiana is so petite that her entire body is the same width as one of my thighs. She has dreadlocks in her hair and she wears them, the dreads, all bunched up and tucked up inside drab colourless ethnic-looking hair-bands. I often wonder why she bothers to hide them away – they take so much trouble to twirl, twist, plait, iron, I can never understand why she doesn't wear them flowing around her shoulders for people to at least see, if not admire.

"Angel, are you listening, can you follow the story that I am telling you about the girl that sells cheese? Don't mind me, my little angel – you won't need to listen to your mum's crazy stories for more than forty-eight hours – this you can be sure of . . . The girl, the Catalan girl, wears those trousers that look like they can't decide whether they are trousers or a skirt. The resulting garment is a baggy oversized crotch that makes up most of her outfit and hides her tiny figure from the world. Her nose is pierced, her lip and her left eyelid too, but not her ears.

"I wonder, if you had made it to this world – when you were big would you too have liked to have all those piercings? I wouldn't mind if you did, if it made you happy, but your dad, I'm not so sure he would approve of it. I would say that he might feel that all the rings in different places would make you imperfect . . . what do you think?

"I always wanted to ask Fabiana why she didn't pierce all those bits that people would normally decorate, like ears. I did think about asking her a few times, but your dad said that she might be insulted by my curiosity, that she might misunderstand me, so I never asked her. He said that she struggled with words as if they, the words, were always fighting with each other.

"Yes, we always enjoyed our trips to the market. We would walk hand in hand back to the apartment with our produce, past the old Georgian tea rooms with their faded blue eaves.

"Fabiana – such a nice name. Angel, now you

need to help me choose a name for you. Have you got any idea what kind of a name you would like? What do you think would suit you? What about Lucy, Lucy with or without an 'e'? Would Lucy suit you – are you a Lucy? Or a Lucey? What do you think?"

I looked down at my rotund belly as if hoping it might answer.

"What about Minnie? What do you think? Might that work well, given that you are going to be so tiny when you are born? Do you think that your dad might like it – Minnie Lynch, Minnie Lynch, Ms Minnie Lynch . . . no, I don't think that really works, does it?"

I used inflection in my voice, to test the name. I spoke it aloud and looked at how my lips said the word in the rear-view mirror. Then I used a different intonation, a sterner one, as if I was reprimanding her. I tried a lower one, as if I was trying to persuade her to do something that she didn't want to do. Then I finished the exercise by using another variation, a whisper. No, it did not sound quite right. It wouldn't do.

Nor could I keep calling her Angel forever. She was an angel, of course, but that was not her name; she needed to be honoured with a name that we had chosen that suited her.

I switched on the radio, low. It was EASY FM. They were still celebrating the Rolling Stones. And they were playing it again, that song.

And I was struck for the first time by the line

where Mick Jagger asks who could hang a name on the girl who comes and goes. Hang a name . . . a girl who comes and goes . . .

"Angel! What do you think of 'Ruby'?" I said in great excitement. "Ruby like the colour of the tree in front of the desk at the window in the bedroom where you were conceived – that tree that your dad calls the 'ruby blossom' or the 'ruby tree' even though I have told him tons of times it's called a cherry blossom. Ruby Lynch . . . will that work . . . will it suit you? Afric, Luke and Ruby Lynch? I think it sounds great. Let's try Ruby for a while and see does it suit you. Right . . . Ruby . . . on we go with our tour! Our next stop will be the East Pier in Dun Laoghaire!"

In the distance there were flashes of colour on the pier, early-morning joggers bouncing up and down on the sea wall.

"Can you see the pier, out there to the right? The East Pier is the one with the bright red lighthouse and the West Pier has the faded green one. If you were ever going to be big, which they say you really don't have much chance of being, you would love the East Pier because right at the end of the pier, just by the lighthouse, is an ice-cream kiosk, and it sells the best ice cream in Ireland. Parents bribe their kids to walk to the end of the pier to get ice cream – it must seem so far for little kids with tiny legs. Then the lovely creamy ice cream is finished, the tears start, and the little legs have to walk all the way back up the pier but without the promise of a special treat at the top.

"Do you know why one pier has a green lighthouse and the other one has a bright red one? Guess why. You don't know? Well, they're not the only red and green lighthouses in Dublin Bay – I bet you thought they were – well, they aren't. The different-coloured lighthouses are to tell the ship where to dock, to park. You see, port means the left side on a ship, starboard means the right side – red is for port and green is for starboard – so as you enter Dun Laoghaire Harbour, if you were a ship, the East Pier and its red lighthouse and red light would be on your left and on the right would be the West Pier with its green lighthouse and light – so the captain would know he was on track. Isn't that cool?

"You know, I don't think I'll go to the East Pier with all its perfect babies any more; it might make me too sad. I'll go to the West Pier in future – anyway the West Pier is better and anyway I prefer green to red."

The water was still like glass. A faint sea mist hung over Seapoint Beach. The tide was going out, so the yellow buoys were tilted on their sides in the water – they looked like drunken old men slumped over.

"The next stop, Ruby, is Sandymount – see there, that is Sandymount." I pointed enthusiastically to the beach.

The tide was so far out you could hardly see any water at all, just an expanse of soggy sand with early Sunday-morning dog walkers that looked like tiny spots on the sand.

I hummed "Goodbye, Ruby Tuesday". "I am gonna miss you, Ruby, like it says in the song. That's your song. Your mum is so silly she didn't make the connection between the song and you until now . . . silly silly Mum."

We stopped outside a dusty pink house. It had steps up to a navy-blue door. The house was surrounded by black railings, which badly needed a lick of paint. In the front garden peach and white roses swayed in the wind. In the corner by the stone wall were the forget-me-not flowers.

"Look, Ruby, the little blue-and-white flowers, the ones with the yellow centres – don't they look like a print from an elegant tea-party set? They are called 'Forget-me-nots'. They are my favourite flower because they are so tiny and so perfect. Henry used to live there in the pink house. He loved travelling and when we were very young he used to go to exotic places like Cairo to sell them seeds for something or other. When I was little I could never understand why he had to take seeds to other countries, why he could not send the seeds on the boat on their own. He explained to me that he had to meet people and tell them how great the seeds were, but I didn't understand that either because wouldn't they see for themselves how good the seeds were when the plants grew? Henry just chuckled to himself when I said that. On a work day he had a lunch box for his sandwiches. When I was little, I always thought it strange that a grown-up had a lunchbox. I thought lunchboxes were only for kids not for big people. Henry's lunch box didn't have any pictures, like Thomas the Tank Engine or Superman, and he didn't have his name on it – he told me he didn't need to put his name on it because he knew what it looked like. Every day, he would sit in Merrion Square on a bench, eat his lunch and read the newspaper. Once he told me that he always sat on the same wooden bench. It has a gold plaque on it, he said, with black writing. He told me it was dedicated to someone, but I didn't really understand what he meant, but I nodded and smiled anyway. I asked him once what would happen if someone was sitting on his bench when he came to eat his lunch. He opened his eyes wide like they might pop out of his head. He said that he would glare at them until they left, but I didn't believe him. He was too kind to glare at strangers so I think he would just smile at them and then go and sit on a different bench.

"When he went on his travels he would bring us back lovely jewelry, like gold rosebud earrings from Cairo – I thought those people in that country must have tiny fingers to be able to make the delicate gold leaves. Another time he brought moonstone rings from exotic Greek Islands and Egyptian bracelets with beautiful intricate designs from old manuscripts.

"He loved good wine and adored great wine – his wife says he spent most of his salary in the wine shop in the village. Henry was a great cook and every Sunday he would cook us all a delicious dinner and serve us plenty of wine. He would phone and say:

'Will I throw you into the pot?' Of course he didn't literally mean that he would throw me into the pot – he was asking me to come to Sunday dinner. He taught me how to pour wine and how to twist the bottle after pouring it – he didn't want to waste a single drop down the side of the bottle."

Early-morning risers were beginning to make their way toward the Sandymount Dart Station; it was after nine thirty on a beautiful summer morning.

We headed down the Grand Canal towards Harold's Cross. The vegetation on either side of the water was lush. People pushed buggies and pulled dogs along the wobbly path that runs alongside the murky brown water of the canal. The water in the canal was low so the riverbed looked like the contents of a skip, with buggies, bikes, shopping trolleys, beer cans and other debris on view from the road.

I was taking my daughter to see the house where I spent ten happy years of life.

"Normally, the canal looks much better than this, Ruby. In its own way it is beautiful, but it is an urban beauty. Sorry you can't see it at a better time," I twittered on.

"There it is, Ruby – see the cottage there with the solid brown door and windows with brown frames – that is our house. I used to live there with my best friend Sue. Imagine having a best friend from the age of four until now! That's thirty-six years – that's a really good return on investment, isn't it? That is a *best* best friend, isn't it? We lived there in that cottage, the two of us. She is a singer and an actress – she's really talented, my little angel, and it's a pity you will never get to meet her, or hear her sing. You would love her. She has eyes the colour of light-blue topaz. I think that she has the most beautiful eyes of any person I have ever met. When you look at her eyes you float away, you get lost – they're like a drug, and they make you dreamy. She's funny too in a really understated way – witty, but without ever being the centre of attention.

"Once she broke her leg. Because she couldn't walk she decided that while the leg was healing she would cycle so that she could get around. So on the street just here, right here where we're parked, we road-tested her cycling with a broken leg. The actual cycling was not the problem – it was getting on and off a man's bike with a crossbar that was the challenge. It was quite an operation to get going. She rested the pedal of the bike on the kerb and then she got on the bike with her good leg still on the pavement so as to balance herself. She took the crutches, pushed in their buttons, shortened them, and then fixed them with an elasticated rope along the bar of the bike, onto the back carrier and over the back mudguard. They stuck out the back of the bike, like fierce artillery. We had tried putting them on the handlebars of the bike but they were too long. We were terrified that they would catch in some granny's Opel Corsa as she drove along the canal looking at the view on a sunny summer afternoon.

"She was fine when she got going; the difficult

part was stopping and starting so we had a few dry runs, right here on the road. Twice she fell off the bike, once because we were laughing so hard. The tears ran down my face as I watched her go up and down the road. But she was so determined that she could do it – you could see it in her focused deep-blue eyes. She was determined to ride that bicycle with a broken leg.

"Then it was time to cycle into town where she was singing at a gig. I offered to drive her, but she was determined to cycle. She was a bit wobbly on the bike, and she decided it safest to stay close to the kerb in the bus lanes. Traffic lights were also a bit of a problem as they involved stopping and starting. Obviously it was best for her to stop at as few sets of lights as possible.

"On the way into town she was weaving in and out of the bus lanes and everything went okay. Then, just near where she was playing her gig, she began to cycle slower so that she wouldn't have to stop at the traffic lights, but the slower pace meant the bike began to wobble. A bus full of passengers swerved to avoid her, and with one big wobble she fell to the ground and the bike fell on top of her.

The bus stopped. All the passengers peered out the window at her on the ground. The alarmed bus driver came running over to her to see if she was okay.

'You okay?' he asked. 'Are you hurt?'

'I don't think so,' she replied. 'Yes, I'm fine – just a bit shocked and I have a broken leg.'

'Ah Jaysus! Not a broken leg! Let me call you an ambulance, love,' and he started to fuss around her.

'No – no need to call an ambulance. I broke my leg weeks ago. I'm fine.'

The intrigued passengers watched from the bus as he helped her to get back up and onto her good foot. She perched herself on the kerb and remounted, with the assistance of the bus driver.

'*Jaysus*, love, I can't believe you're cycling with a broken leg! Why don't you get the bus?'

'Hadn't thought of it – maybe next time.'

The people on the bus watched the girl with a broken leg cycle off. Sue said she wondered how many people on that bus were at her gig. She hoped a few so that they could say that they'd been properly entertained."

Chapter 7

I reversed a little down the street, away from the white cottage. I was afraid that the girl who had rented our cottage would think that the owner was spying on her.

"When your dad first moved to Dublin, we lived here for two years; they were the best two years of our life together. By then Sue had moved to New York where she joined a funky jazz band. Your dad, when he was young, lived in a house with a garden on a big farm in the countryside. The cottage has only two small bedrooms, a tiny kitchen and small bathroom. It has no garden. Your dad often said it was like living on the street and sleeping with four other people. You could hear how the neighbours on each side lived their lives. When they argued we would both takes sides in their disputes, and then we would end up fighting too – it was all a bit mad. He felt that he was three sizes too big for the cottage – he banged his head on the door frames and kept knocking things over. There's a flat roof on the bathroom, and during our first hot summer he would climb up the ladder and sunbathe naked on the flat roof. The hot tar of the roof would stick to his bum but he didn't care – he was desperate for sun. He would look up at the clouds and say he felt like Chicken Licken, afraid that the sky might fall down on him. He said the clouds were too close to his head, that the winter gave him claustrophobia.

"Shh, my little girl, please don't kick me – quiet now – the whirlwind tour won't take much longer. Are you enjoying it, my little girl?

"We would cycle around the city for hours. I would give him guided tours telling him all sorts of ridiculous stories about Irish myths. I made up half of them because I could only recall bits of the legends. He would try to read the signs in Irish – he never quite got the pronunciation correct – he even struggled with Irish place names – Port Laoise he would pronounce like Port Louis, making it sound like some exotic Caribbean island instead of the town that was home to the largest prison in Ireland.

"You see, Ruby, my hope was that he would fall madly in love with Ireland and with me and he would never want to leave. I wanted him to move here, forever. I focused all my attention for that one year on taking him to the most beautiful spots in Ireland. We went to Connemara in winter, when it was covered in snow, with clear blue skies. We stayed in a beautiful handcrafted wooden lodge overlooking a lake and watched the sun set on the snow, the evening sun turning the snow pink. It was magical.

"We climbed Croagh Patrick on a day you could see every single island in Clew Bay it was so clear – you know, Clew Bay has an island for every day of the year. On a freezing October day we swam down through the mussel beds in Killary Fjord, with the burnt autumn reds and oranges on the trees and the baldy-headed mountain behind. We emerged frozen and exhausted and drank hot whiskeys until our frostbite thawed.

"We swam in luxurious swimming pools in castle hotels that had their coat of arms tiled on the bottom of the pool. We sat in a bubbling hot outdoor Jacuzzi on a freezing November evening sipping pints of Guinness overlooking the Lakes of Killarney, with desolate snow-clad mountain tops in the distance. We swam around the Aran Islands in summer. 'But they didn't look that big on the map, they were only dots,' he said, having been stung by jelly fish, chased by seals and battered by the Atlantic Ocean. After each adventure we would return to the little cottage, exhausted and exhilarated, craving the next outing together.

"We had the best sex, but I don't want to tell you about that. I don't think that a mother ever really discusses her sex life with her daughter, does she? I don't think so.

"Then, after six months, I knew that he was hooked. At the beginning I was never too sure if he was keen on your mother or Ireland or a bit of both. He no longer talked of returning home; instead he began to call Dublin his home. My task was complete. Maybe that is what happened, Ruby – maybe because I thought I had him then I became complacent.

"We would drive out to Dublin Bay and swim for miles. Then wrapped in warm layers and semi-frozen we would stop for a creamy pint of Guinness and a packet of Tayto on the way home. On very cold days your dad would wear his slippers. Then Tommy, the fella behind the bar, would look at us when we walked in the door. His greeting to us was always 'Jaysus, don't tell me that you were at that craic again? Have ye no sense?' Your dad would perch himself up at the bar and chat to Tommy. Tommy would say, 'And you're not even from here and you have less sense'. To Tommy that was a compliment. He would tell your dad stories about the fishermen of Dun Laoghaire and stories of Dublin Bay. Then we would come back to our tiny terraced cottage, perished and refreshed.

"Your dad is a fabulous swimmer, you know, but he had never really been a sea swimmer – too many sharks where he comes from. He loved the idea of being able to finish work and then jump in the sea and swim for miles. We became addicted to sea swimming; we swam for hours and hours side by side in Dublin Bay, often just the two of us gliding through the water. We would stop in the middle of the bay, relaxed and in love. 'How happy are we?' he would often say. 'Aren't we are the luckiest people on this planet?' I would reply: 'Yes, I would say we are.' We'd swim side by side, breathing to the left, seeing views of the Head of Howth, with its vibrant yellow gorse-clad hills. 'Doesn't the gorse cheer up those hills?' he would say. Further down the headland from the patches of golden bushes the white-and-grey lighthouse sat on a lonely rock with the sea crashing up on it. Some days, I would say to your dad: 'Today the water is flirting with the rocks.' Other days it was as if they were raging with each other – other times they seemed just like friends that were getting on.

"Then we would breathe to the right and see the DART race past, packed with commuters. From the sea, the carriages looked like mass-produced items on a conveyor belt whizzing by. Just above the DART line was a solid line of different-coloured rectangular objects: it was the rush-hour traffic jam snaking along the coast road – more commuters, just in a different race.

"Often when we stopped at the end of our lap we would look up and watch a plane come in over Howth Head, in towards Dublin Bay. We would guess where the plane was coming from; it was a silly game that we would play. We would dream about where we would go if we had all the money in the world. We would always choose locations surrounded by water, exotic locations where we could swim, snorkel and dive all day, where the sky was high.

"One day, in the middle of Dublin Bay, I asked your dad, if he could choose one place for that plane to take him, anywhere in the world, where would it be? Do you know what he said, Ruby? Right there in the middle of the Irish Sea. He took off his goggles, placed them on the front of his swimming cap, continued to tread water and said: 'I would get that plane to turn around and go right back to Dublin airport because there is nowhere in the whole world I would prefer to be than right here with you.' My heart nearly melted, though my body was frozen by the temperature of the water. 'Afric,' he said, 'never in my life have I ever been so happy, I mean really happy.' Then he said: 'I love you, I want to be with you forever and ever, and never let you go.'

I looked down at my bump and rubbed it gently.

"Yes, Ruby, that is what he said. I was speechless, both from the cold and the shock. And do you want to know what he said next? I must tell you this. He said: 'Please marry me and we will spend our days together swimming. Marry me and I will take you to swim in every ocean in the world – that is my promise to you if you marry me: every ocean in the world. Marry me, please, Afric.' And, Ruby, guess what your mother did, guess what I did . . . I burst out crying and the tears flowed down my cheeks and into the sea. Luke just treaded water beside me, looking at me, waiting for an answer. 'Luke,' I replied, 'yes, of course I will, yes, of course I will marry you.' Then, Ruby, he took me in his arms, and the rubber of our suits clung to each other. Treading water, he took my face and cupped it in his hands. He traced his finger along my lower lip and kissed me very tenderly in the middle of Dublin Bay. Behind us a huge Irish Ferries ferry with its bright red masts chugged its way into Dublin Port, the DART whizzed by, the traffic piled up, and yachts sailed past us. Ruby, isn't that so romantic? Isn't it like a fairy tale? He used to call me his Irish mermaid . . . but he has not said those words in so long, in so very long – in fact I had almost forgotten he used to call me that."

I was beginning to feel movement just below my belly button. I checked the time on the clock: **10.38 a.m.**

"That should be my aim, to get our relationship back on track – aim for him to call me his Irish mermaid once more. Oh Ruby, you must not worry about your mum and dad – we are fine – well, what I mean is we will be fine – we're just going through a rocky patch. I guess the secret is for the rocky patch to be just short term, to get over it, identify why it was rocky and move on. That is what I am going to do the next time he is home. When he gets back from China, we will sit down together, the two of us, just Luke and me, and work it out – find out what the problem is and we'll find a solution. We're only slightly derailed, that's all. We'll sort it out, we'll get back on track, move on and relearn how to love each other, relearn how to make each other laugh, laugh out loud. That is what I'll do when he comes home, when you are gone. I couldn't bear to lose you both, to lose both people I love so dearly. How terrible would that be? Yes, it is up to me to fix it, to rekindle our love. It just needs a bit more attention; we need to pay our relationship more attention. Otherwise he might become very sad again; the deep sadness might return. I need to make him the most important thing in my life, like before. Maybe I can just replace you with him, do a kind of a swop, swop you for your dad.

"Oh, Ruby, sometimes I say the silliest things that are totally inappropriate. Nothing, of course, my darling, will ever replace you – nothing. What I am trying to say is if I bundle up all the love that I have for you and just transfer it directly on to your dad, then maybe that might fix our relationship. What do you think? Would that work? Probably I'm not paying him enough attention – you know how high maintenance men are – well, you don't really, and you never will. God, maybe you're lucky to be saved that trouble – men are like cats – they need loads of attention and love. They need to be told how fantastic they are every single day."

My phone blipped. It read: **1 New Message.**

I checked it.

Morning, Afric, love you, miss you, safe journey today, call me when you arrive in Liverpool Xx

I responded with an 'X'. Now was not a time for a Yes-No conversation. I was busy on our outing which I thought was going very well.

"Yes, my angel, we both worked hard at our jobs. Our careers – they became our lives, our focus. Your dad travelled and I moulded my own life around his absence. We sort of forgot about our marriage and that is when we started to drift apart. We were both hoping that when you were born it would somehow make it all okay – you would arrive like a miracle cure and it all would be okay. Silly, I know, my little angel. That is a lot of pressure to put on a newborn baby, isn't it? I mean, you just arrive into the world, and you are not even well and already you're supposed to fix your parents' marriage. Crazy, I know, Ruby, just crazy. But you know one thing: I know we can fix it because deep down we are still in love with each other – it's just that the love is a little too deep down to access on a daily basis. We need to bring it closer to the surface so that it can become something that we can touch every day and always and not just for special occasions.

"When you get up there in the sky, in a couple of days, you might help us with that, would you? As your first job it's not that bad a job, is it?"

I felt a slight sensation, like a mini-cramp on the right-hand side of my stomach. She was on the move again, or else she was acknowledging that she had heard her mum. I looked down at her.

"I am sorry that you will never have the chance to fall in love, for someone to hold you really tight, that feeling of holding someone really close to you. I am so sorry that you will never know that gushing feeling, butterflies in your stomach, that intense love. Your dad and I once had it, but now it feels like so long ago. We were so in love, we were each other's world. Definitely, my little girl, that is your first job up in heaven: please give us a hand to get back on track.

"Your dad wanted a bigger house – the cottage

started to annoy him. He kept saying it was too small for modern living. For a while I didn't understand what he meant by that, but in hindsight he meant he wanted to have a home for better dinner parties, for kids and a dog, more of everything. He wanted it not just for him – he wanted it for us, for you and me. He wanted to give his wife and kids a good life with the best of everything. Every man wants to provide the best he can for his family and your dad is no different. You see, in his head there is this perfect world that he is striving every day to attain. Every new international client, every overseas conference is getting him one step closer to his dream."

Chapter 8

"Ruby, we need to get moving – we have to say a last goodbye to the cottage, and we have one more stop to make."

I indicated and pulled out on to Canal Road. Cars, bikes, motorbikes and power-walking commuters hurried down the canal – like a herd of cows, they all moved in the same direction, only at different speeds.

"I would say that it is entirely my fault that he is insecure – maybe because I don't tell him how wonderful he is. Girly magazines always have articles about how the modern man feels less valued in the world today, that he is no longer sure of what his role is. They say he feels confused, undervalued. I always thought those articles were total trash, but maybe they are correct, perhaps the modern man is in crisis, maybe your dad is just longing for me to say: 'You know what, Luke, I don't need a flashy car, a big house or a posh school for our child.' Should I say that to him? Yes, Ruby, when he comes back, I will tell him just that.

"Then in 2010 your dad got a great job in Ireland. It was the middle of the recession, so there were not too many jobs to choose from. When we read the job spec we both agreed that it was far too much travelling, but we convinced each other that as soon as he got the job we could change that, we could change the way a soulless multinational operated. We were so naïve – because once he was in there, there was no escaping. The trips got more frequent and longer and longer – trips to China and Dubai that the more senior consultants didn't want. You see, part of the problem was that for the first six months he was on probation, so he had no choice but to travel. Then, because he was so successful and won new lucrative Asian and Middle Eastern clients, the demanding new customers wanted to deal only with him, and it became a vicious circle. As the international clients grew, so too did the profits from the honey-pots of Asia. Then it became a cycle of winning more clients; days of being away from home became weeks. Your dad travelled for work a lot more than we both had expected. He either spent weekends away, or at the end of the week he was recovering from jet lag, or sleeping in an effort to help him make it through the next gruelling and demanding week that lay ahead. You see, Ruby, China was now the world's power house and that was where Sheppard Consulting – that is who your dad works for – that was where they wanted their muscle, there at the coalface, minding and growing their international consultancy business. A successful stint in the ferocious Chinese market place could later be rewarded with an easier number in the domestic market. Or so they had told him. So that is how it happened, how we started to grow apart, ever so slowly. I went into default position and very simply went back to my single days – all the girls still hung out together and welcomed me back with open arms."

The early-morning traffic on the canal this morning didn't seem as frantic as normal, but of course I had forgotten it was a Sunday and most commuters were safely tucked under their duvets.

"Yes, I missed your dad a lot at the beginning, an awful lot in fact, but then I just got used to it. Funny how you can train yourself to adapt to anything. I wonder, Ruby, how long it will take me to train myself to forget you. Will I ever forget you? I wonder how long it will take for me not to rub my stomach and realise that it is empty and you are gone, and with you all our dreams and hopes of the future. How long will it take for my swollen empty stomach to recede and hopefully with it some of the pain? My little angel, I dread the pain and the hurt so much. Will I ever be happy again after you have gone, will I ever laugh out loud? How will I carry on?"

My eyelids began to tremble and I could feel my eyes filling with tears. No, I told myself, no tears on our outing. I swallowed hard and tried to dismiss the morbid thoughts.

When an old person dies, you mourn the past, the loss of their life. But I was mourning the future, because I was losing my vision of the future. Was I going to be stuck in this moment of my life forever because there was no future any more? It had been robbed from me, the future, and nothing, absolutely nothing could ever bring it back. It was as though my own body had betrayed me, had sold me out. How was it possible that Luke's and my flesh could allow us to create something that was incompatible with life?

I was angry at my own being, it had betrayed me, and it had created this present and future pain. I felt scared about what was to come.

"I'm losing your dad, but hopefully not to that awful sadness, and now I am losing you – tomorrow you will be gone." I swallowed very hard and scolded myself: "Afric, stop that, stop being so selfish! You will upset the child with that self-pity. Get a grip."

I opened all the windows of the car to let the words and pain escape and to let the fresh air in. I took big deep breaths, the type that I should have learnt at ante-natal classes.

Ruby was kicking. I looked down at my swollen stomach. "Please, darling, don't kick me so hard – shh, my baby, just wait for ten minutes and we'll be at the Great South Wall. We'll go for a walk along the wall and then you'll drift off to sleep again. Just a few more minutes, my darling. Look there!" I pointed directly ahead of me. "Can you see the towers over there? See the white-and-red ones stretching towards the clouds. Please stop moving so much, it makes me very uncomfortable. Soon you won't be kicking. In fact you will never kick again. Is that why you're using your legs right now, is it? To show me that they work, to prove to me that you have two legs? Are you trying to tell me that you're fine? I wish you were fine, little girl, but you are not. You are a very sick girl."

With one hand I guided the car towards the Pigeon House, the other hand on my bump.

"See it there – the old generating station. We are nearly there. The Poolbeg Lighthouse is at the end of the Great South Wall – that is where we're going, did I tell you that? Did you know that the lighthouse was lit by candles once upon a time? Imagine how big those candles must have been for the ships to be able to see them. They must have been huge, really huge, for the boats to be able to see the flame. Now we are nearly there – shh, my little angel, just two more minutes." I rubbed my belly in clockwise circles to try to calm my baby. "Shh, baby, it's sleepy time."

Ruby's response was to just kick harder and harder. I didn't want to correct her again because, after all, it was her day out too. Maybe she was telling me that she was enjoying it.

"The girls, you know, us girlfriends, we would text each other: **Want to walk the wall?** It was kind of a secret code for 'I have something to tell you', or

119

a bit of gossip, or 'I need to talk'. I have walked this wall so often – it must be a few hundred times. Funny, it is one of the walks that I never did on my own. Strange how some walks are just your walks, like the West Pier in Dun Laoghaire is just my walk – I don't like sharing that walk really with anyone else – it's a place of solitude for just me and my thoughts, a place to get my head clear, to organise my thinking. Here is different. It's a walk that I always associate with my girlfriends, and that is why I brought you here because you are my little girlfriend, so I wanted to walk it just once with you. So it is good that I'm not walking it alone, that we are together. Ruby, are you listening to your mother? Do you hear me? Your mother is talking to you. This wall has heard lots of my stories. It's a place where you can tell a secret, or make a confession, because here on the wall you know that your confession or secret is safe, you know that it will be swept away by the Irish sea air. So now I have walked this wall on the saddest day of my life. And on the happiest or nearly the happiest. The second happiest day of my life was the day I got engaged to your dad, the happiest the day I married him. After he proposed to me in Seapoint, we got into the car, drove here and walked the wall.

"It was a cold spring day, there was not a cloud in the sky, and cherry blossom was just appearing on the trees. Like I told you before, he could never remember the correct name – he always got it wrong and called it 'ruby blossom' or the 'ruby tree' – he always said that the colour was nearer to ruby than cherry and anyway he preferred the name. So from then on we always called it 'ruby blossom'. He said that one day when we got our own house we would have a huge ruby-blossom tree in the garden. It was a clear cool day in April, and he held my hand tight as we walked the wall. So I think that Luke will like the name Ruby – I think he will be pleased with the name: Ruby . . . Ruby Lynch.

"It was right here that we planned to swim every inch of Dublin Bay – that is a lot of swimming, you know, because Dublin Bay is a C-shaped bay – it's ten kilometres at its widest and seven kilometres in length. I told him that if that was true we were going to be in the water for a long time. See, Ruby, from here, standing on the wall, is the only place in Dublin that you can see every inch of Dublin Bay, this spot right here."

A breeze blew over the pier, sending ripples down the sea like a shiver.

"Are you warm enough, darling? I will zip up my jacket to keep you snug. It's not so warm out of the sun, is it? You okay now? Warm enough? That's a good girl now, time for bed, time for your morning nap.

"Before I met your dad, the girls and your mum would trawl the holiday websites for late offers. We would spend hours online, eating pistachios and sipping white wine, looking for the most exotic and adventurous holidays at rock-bottom prices. We had the process down to a fine art. We signed up for alerts from holiday websites, asking them to only send us information when the holiday price fell below five hundred euros. We would call up cruise companies and enquire for last-minutes deals, availing of inside cabins that often remained unsold. Nearer holiday time, on Friday lunchtimes we would call tour operators that had package holidays departing that Saturday, and haggle and try to buy the last-minute departures at knockdown prices. 'We don't care where we go,' we would tell the travel agents. 'Bed and beach is all we need: Turkey, Greece, Spain or Portugal.' We would tell them that we would get the culture from the local yoghurt."

I touched my belly very softly. She had drifted off to sleep. I would get to walk the wall, together with her, but alone with my memories.

"Ruby, the thrill was to try to find the most luxurious holiday at the cheapest price. Just after 9/11 struck, your mum did in-depth research into Greek Islands that wealthy Americans visited. Patmos, I discovered, was a favourite with Yanks from the East Coast of the States. For seven days we whizzed around an almost deserted and idyllic Greek island on battered old mopeds. By day we swam in the crystal-clear waters of the Aegean Sea and in hidden white sandy coves. By night we partied in the local town of Skala and drank ouzo and the local white wine by the gallon. The wine we nicknamed 'Ratsemen' because of its foul taste and the horrific hangover." I rubbed my black fleece. "That's my girl, stay asleep now. In our empty luxury boutique hotel, we enjoyed long liquid lunches munching on unidentifiable seafood. Late in the afternoon, sun-kissed and exhausted, we would float to the swim-up bar, perch ourselves on the edge of the pool and drink cocktails. Every day a different-coloured cocktail until we had reached the bottom of the cocktails menu, then we started at the top again. When the sun had set and our skin was wrinkled from the water we would haul ourselves reluctantly from the pool. Then came 'girly hour' as we called it. It involved getting ready to go out on the town for the night. But, as Aoife pointed out, 'Who are we getting ready for? There's no chance of landing a rich Yank! There's no one on the island but ourselves and the locals! We're here because the wealthy Americans aren't!' But that didn't matter; we all agreed that 'girly hour' was far too therapeutic to get rid of. Skin soothed with one-hundred-per-cent aloe vera, we would convince each other that we deserved a full body massage followed by a make-up session sipping early-evening gin and tonics."

We had almost reached the end of the sea wall. From here the sea cliffs looked much more sheer and the fields on the headland were a deeper green. Today, the lighthouse and the sea were best friends.

"Do you see the red lighthouse there, Ruby? It's much bigger than the one near where we live, isn't it? This one is really fancy; it even has steps that wind the whole way to the top."

I had forgotten, distracted by my own stories – I had forgotten she was sleeping.

Tears welled up in my eyes and I blinked hard to hold them back. I dug my nails firmly into the palms of my hands and looked straight ahead of me, out on the calm blue sea. It was beautiful June morning. The sea was flat, the sky cloudless. But even the tranquil sea was not enough to calm me.

"Today, my little angel, is the saddest day of my life. What could be more heartbreaking than taking my sick little girl on a whirlwind tour of my life, visiting very special places and memories of people? It's devastating to know that it is only your poor deformed body and your racing heart that are with me."

I struggled to control my feelings. I must not spoil the tour for her.

"Ruby, it's time to remember the happier days I had walking here, when we were laughing so much that the other walkers would smile as they passed us by. Tortured couples would grimace in envy, wishing they too could share in our hilarity and be dragged away from day-to-day humdrum life, if only for a while. One of the funniest days was when I told the girls the 'bus story'. Will I tell it to you, Ruby? This is the last story that I will tell you on the wall."

I turned and strolled back up the wall in the direction of Dublin Port. To my left the Sugarloaf majestically peered over Dublin Bay and early-morning sailors cheered up the sea with their coloured sails. Dublin Bay had never looked so good; it was as though it was putting on its very best performance for our day out.

"Just after my thirtieth birthday, so that is ten years ago, I was stuck in a rut in my life. Everything was fine, just ticking along, but there was nothing wildly exciting or particularly fantastic to entertain me. I decided, as they say, to 'get a life'. I thought that I should fall madly in love, so I tried that but found no one fantastic to fall madly in love with. I concluded that I was more attracted to the idea of being in love than to finding the right person. Eventually, I parked the idea of falling in love. Instead I would take a year out and head off and travel. Gladly I gave up my well-paid, steady job, and borrowed a pile of cash from the bank. I decided to go to South America. I would begin my travels in Buenos Aires and travel anti-clockwise around the continent, arriving back in Buenos Aires a year later. I would of course be both inspired and invigorated by my journey. I might even eventually figure out what I wanted to do with the rest of my life. I bet, Ruby, you're thinking how crazy your mum is."

I looked down at my protruding belly. My little girl was still fast asleep – she must like the stories and the stroll.

"My intention was to travel overland on buses. There they have great buses that are very luxurious, with seats that at night become comfortable beds. I would sleep and travel by night and by day walk, hike, cycle, swim and ski. Did you know there are fifteen different countries on the continent? Fifteen was too many to get around, so I selected seven or eight for my visit."

A tall skinny man, slightly stooped over, appeared from behind me. As he passed me he called out: "Beautiful morning!" Off he went, bouncing up and down in a high visibility vest.

"Are you listening, Ruby? Listen because it's the last story. Where was I? Yes, my travelling plan worked just fine a lot of the time. However, as I travelled through Venezuela towards the Brazilian border, getting around began to get more difficult because the area around the Amazon basin is so remote. The roads have potholes as big as craters, there are no signs on the roads, and the bus rarely comes – a bit like Ireland, I suppose. I needed to get from a place called Santa Elena de Uairen – that's on the Great Plain of Venezuela, in the jungle, and in that jungle you can't walk so only the animals can go there – I had to get from there to Manaus in the Amazon Basin. You know, Ruby, the Amazon is the second longest river in the world. Did you know that?"

I looked down at her but she didn't respond, so I continued on with my story.

"I waited a day for a comfortable bus to come along but there was not another one due for two days, so I got on an ordinary bus. No beds on this bus. It was made for tiny people and my legs didn't fit in the seats – I stretched them out in the narrow aisles. There was a huge mirror at the front of the bus, to the right of the bus driver's head, so that he could see all the people on the bus. The journey was going to take eighteen hours on this boneshaker. Do you know what the Venezuelans call those buses? They call them 'Aspirins', because when you get off the bus you have to take two aspirins to get rid of the pain in your head from all the rattling.

"When I got on, the bus was very busy with lots of people going from Venezuela to Brazil. They thought that I was an alien – I mean, from outer space – you see, Ruby, in other countries people are not used to seeing freckles and reddish-brown hair. Because I had been in the sun so long, all my freckles were stuck together so I had groups of freckles on my face, especially on my lips and my eyelids. They looked – the freckles – as though they had bumped into one another, the groups of freckles.

"Do you know, Ruby, that your dad has heaps and heaps of freckles too. And so does your gran, Lizzy. That is a lot of freckles, must be hundreds of thousands of them, for just one family. Funny, isn't it, how Ireland has so many freckles and such a big country like Bolivia doesn't have any – seems unfair, doesn't it – given that freckles are such beautiful things? You see, the thing about freckles is that they are hereditary. Do you know what that means? Do you, Ruby? Well, what it means is that if someone in your immediate family has something, like red hair or freckles, then you are likely to have them too.

"When they told me you were incompatible with life, I was afraid that it was something hereditary – that you got it from us. I mean, you did get it from us cos we created you – but I thought it was genetic – that it came from our genes – but it isn't genetic. So maybe someday we might try again – for another you but a different one – one that is compatible with life.

"Oh yes, I was telling you about the Argentineans – they call freckles 'kisses from God' – isn't that a lovely saying? And do you know that once when I was on a bus in Bolivia a little girl, only about seven, came and sat on the seat next to me. For the first while she just stared at me, from my toes to the top of my head, then her confidence grew and she stretched out her small sallow-skinned index finger. Very slowly her finger approached the back of my hand. Lightly, she tapped the freckles there. I smiled down at her and she started to giggle. Then with the same finger she repeated the exercise but this time she rubbed my freckles a bit harder. Her deep-brown eyes looked down at her little finger. Slowly she turned her fingertip so that it looked up at her, but the freckles were not on the top of her finger. Her eyes looked sad. Then she looked at me, and in Spanish she said: 'Can you please give me just one freckle? You have lots and my mummy has none. I would like to give her just one of yours.' I told her that they don't come off. She said 'Okay' but I knew it was not, that she didn't believe me. I wonder, if you were not fatally sick, would you have had freckles and reddish-brown hair like your mum, or would you have your dad's beautiful chocolate-brown eyes, like a Dairy Milk Chocolate bar? I wonder would you have been like him, cool, calm and kind. Your dad is a good man, Ruby, a very good, kind man.

"Sorry, I'm rambling again – oh, the bus, yes, the

bus story. I was on the bus, just smiling back at all the staring eyes. I took out my book, water and sleeping bag and settled in for an eighteen-hour journey. After a few hours I was awoken by a big jerk forward. We had run out of road and were travelling down a dried-up riverbed of the Amazon. I needed now to go to the loo. The bus driver looked at me as I stood up. I felt like an oversized giant. I smiled at him but thought it would be better if he concentrated on the road, instead of on me. I waddled down the bus, trying to avoid bumping off the passengers seated on the aisle. I opened the door of the chemical toilet. It was filthy, but filthy or not I had to go. I locked the door from the inside. There was no question of actually sitting on the bowl. I hovered over it, trying to steady myself over the toilet before I actually used it. No wonder the bloody thing was so filthy. There was a loud bang on the door. I opened it to a tiny shrivelled-up lady who blabbered something, with emphatic gestures, about not using the toilet now, because the road for the next while was very bumpy."

We had nearly reached the end of the wall. I looked at my watch. It was 11.06, and my companion on the wall was still fast asleep. She felt lifeless.

"I thanked her for her concern; she seemed surprised when I answered her in Spanish. I closed the door. Not wanting to touch anything in the toilet, I rolled my sundress right up and tucked it in securely under my bra. I repeated the exercise at the back, shoving my dress up firmly under my bra strap. The Aspirin bus was wobbling like hell and it jumped each time it struck a pothole. I gripped the handrails and, with my bum poised ready to pee, I tried to align myself with the toilet bowl. I squatted down even further to get closer to the bowl. I was just about to relieve myself when the bus hit a huge crater in the road. I was flung to the left, my elbow banged down on the handle of the unlocked door, the door flung open and I crashed down on the aisle of the bus.

"There I lay in shock with my dress firmly tucked underneath my bra, pretty much entirely naked for the entire bus to see. I looked up and all the eyes on the bus were staring at me in complete amazement. For the passengers who didn't have the pleasure of seeing the fall, they got the second half of the action in the huge mirror as I struggled to remove my dress from my bra. By now I thought my bladder was going to explode. I crawled like a beaten animal on my hands and knees back into the toilet cubicle, where I began once again the process of trying to use the toilet at the bottom of the Amazon basin.

"Maybe, Ruby, it is just as well that you never got to know your crazy mother. I wonder who you would have been like – would you have been sporty and adventurous like your mum? Or would you have been more creative with your hands like your dad? Or maybe you would have been musical. Your dad claims he can sing but, having listened to him in the shower, honestly he is not up to much. Or you might

have been completed different from us both and just
been your own person." I would never know.

I opened the car door. It was 11:38, and we were
running slightly over schedule, though still on time.

We passed the Shelley Banks, where kite-surfers
looked unhappily at the calm seas. In the distance the
East and West Piers stood stately in Dublin Bay.

"Wave bye to the piers, to the coloured lighthouses,
Ruby!"

But she didn't hear me, she was fast asleep. Our
whirlwind tour was nearly complete. We drove away
from the stone pier with the red lighthouse. We left
Dublin Bay and the lighthouses in the rear-view
mirror, forever.

"Do you know that I often know what your dad
is thinking by what he sings in the shower? Often he
sings 'I Love You, Baby'. But his favourite song is
'Let's Get It On' – that means he's looking for love –
before he started working abroad he would sing it
aloud at least twice a day. I would run around the
house to get away from his constant demand for love
and attention. When he isn't singing, I get worried.
Your dad doesn't sing when he's very sad, Ruby. I
don't think he will sing for a long time after you have
gone, maybe never, but I hope he will sing again
some time, some day. That's another job for you
when you're up in the sky: to encourage your dad to
sing again. I know you're asleep, but you can hear
me, can't you?"

I flung the change into the coin basket and the
red-and-white barrier flew up.

"That's the Liffey we're crossing now – it's the river in the middle of Dublin city, so it's not very clean. It's the river that your dad races down every year. You know that for every mouthful of water you swallow during the race, you have to drink a full pint of Guinness to kill all the bad stuff in the water. Every year he swallows more and more water.

"Ruby, look there, to the right out the window. Do you see over there, the bird right there, perched on the top of the bridge, the one with the red beak and red feet? Can you see how the top half of its head is black and the bottom half below the beak is white? That bird is called an 'Arctic Tern' – watch it fly and then glide. Those are my favourite birds – they fly from one end of the world to the other and back again in just one year. Imagine that! Flying over forty thousand kilometres a year. Do you know why I love them? Because they follow the sun – they see more sunlight than any other creatures in the world – they are called 'the bird of the sun', and they remind me of your dad and his need for sunlight. They stop in Dublin for a little city break on their way around the world – they seem to like it here.

"Hang on now, my little girl, don't be scared – we're going to head into the tunnel – it will be darker than normal in my tummy, but don't be scared – Mum will look after you.

"Your dad grew up in the sunshine and he really misses it, so he always says when we win the lotto we will follow the sun. Then I told him about the Arctic Tern one day when we were walking the wall and he told me that he believed in reincarnation. Before, he wanted to come back as a dog, as a chow with a black tongue and white fur, but now he wants to come back as an Arctic Tern and fly and glide around the world following the sun.

"I wonder after tomorrow, Ruby, will you come back as a bird of the sun? What do you think? Who are you going to come back as? Are you going to come back to look after us? To make sure that your dad won't be sad forever?"

Chapter 9

"Is it just yourself?" the young pimply check-in guy enquired.

I looked around me as if I expected someone else to appear.

"Yes," I responded. "I'm travelling alone."

He looked down at my bump and back up at me.

"Will I give you an emergency-exit seat? Are you fit and healthy?"

"Yes, yes, thank you, I am," I lied.

I slid into my seat in the emergency-exit row by the window.

They have a look on this low-cost airline, I thought. The boys are skinny and sallow-skinned and their hair is so gelled that it stands up, dead straight. Their male waists are a size zero. They are overzealous and super-beautiful as if constantly posing for the annual charity calendar. There is now a low-cost speak too that is used on all flights and for all announcements. There are no full stops or commas, not even a breath of air is taken – any pausing is simply time-wasting. All the sentences flow into each other: the announcements are one long unintelligible sentence.

"God, Ruby, wouldn't you hate to think what might happen during an emergency?" I whispered to her. "When they all reverted to their native languages chaos would ensue and they would all fix their hair for the emergency landing. You know, the sales pitch would probably still go on – no doubt the emergency drill would include selling smokeless cigarettes to calm the customers as the plane nose-dived. Well, Ruby, this is the only way to get to Liverpool so we don't have much of a choice and if it's any consolation you're on a one-way ticket."

Over the last couple of days I had become an expert at avoiding all types of eye contact. Once you do it a few times, it becomes quite easy. You don't want to be blatantly rude either. There is an art to it. You look over someone. It's as though you're looking at their face, but you are in fact looking at the top of the back of their head but from the front. You see just beyond them. Eye contact can open up a series of uncomfortable questions, eye contact can tell too much.

I put on my head phones and closed my eyes. I dozed off, feeling tired after our early-morning outing.

I woke having slept for only fifteen minutes

though it felt like I had been sleeping for hours. I sat up and looked around, afraid I had been dribbling or snoring or both.

Her squinty eyes and cold-steel gaze felt as though they were going to pierce every bone of my body. She glared out of the corners of her eyes. The small wiry woman frowned at my stomach, then at my face, then moved on to my eyes and then back down at my bulge. Her watery dull-brown eyes and her mean lips were invading my space. She had wavy dull-brown hair and plum-coloured lipstick that was plastered just outside the outline of her lips. She was dressed in a light beige suit with a plain off-white blouse. A remarkably unspectacular outfit, I thought. Her outfit matched her personality, as I was about to find out, devoid of colour and life.

I closed my eyes to avoid engaging with her but I was too late: eye contact had been stolen from me by her. She was in. I had made another fatal mistake.

"Off to Liverpool then?" she chirped.

"Yes," I replied, trying to shut off the conversation.

"For just a couple of days? Meeting someone, are you?"

"Yes," I replied to her second and third questions. "Yes, I am meeting people there."

Yes-No answers were not going to deter this woman. She seemed like a professional. I suspected that she was an expert at sucking information from vulnerable bodies. The parasitic type. My mother's words rang in my ears – she always told us, "Have respect for your elders", "Be polite" and her favourite was "It is nice to be nice."

"Oh, that will be nice. Have you ever been to Liverpool before? Great city, you know, lots of shopping, lovely restaurants and some great disco bars too. Or so they tell me. They say that the nightlife is the best – well, you would easily know by the tiny little skirts that they wear – so short and you know they even wear them in the middle of winter – it's a wonder that they don't get pneumonia. I'd say half of them have kidney infections except they are so cold and drunk they don't even know it." She appeared relieved now that she had got that rant out of the way.

I fixed my gaze just above her head, pursed my lips and nodded my head. "I know," I replied. I could think of nothing more to say.

"I suppose you won't see much of the nightlife in your condition!" She giggled to herself aloud, as though not including me in our conversation. "You can't keep going for long these days, I suppose? But still, even in your condition it's nice to get a break, isn't it? So where did you say you were staying?"

"I'm going to a conference – an IT conference." I hoped that by providing all the essential information in a single statement she would be both satisfied and disappointed with my story.

"Oh, I see, that will be nice, won't it?" Either she was softening a little or more likely she hadn't got the faintest idea what the IT bit meant – I mean, how could an IT conference be nice – nicely dull perhaps!

"Yes," I said. "I'm going with Ruby." The words

were out and the ball was back in her court now – not what I wanted.

I fixed my eyes on the white tissue paper on the headrest of the seat directly in front of me. I dug my nails firmly into the palm of my hand, and blinked. Maybe she did see the tears well up in my eyes – because the questioning eased. Maybe she did have a gentle heart and just a bad manner. I gave her half a smile.

"Ruby . . . that's a strange name," she continued after a while. "I mean, would it not be a bit odd to be called after jewelry? I am never sure about that name and it's becoming very common these days . . . Ruby . . . Ruby . . ." Her voice petered out.

The plane rattled as we touched down in Liverpool Airport, an announcement about arriving before landing time filled the aircraft, and the air stewards fixed their hair. We ground to a screeching halt. Ruby and I were jolted forward and then back. The rubbish was collected in a fierce hurry. Mobiles were switched on before the seatbelt sign was off, so there was another near-unintelligible announcement scolding the bold passengers. Then the fumbling of looking for bags overhead and under seats began.

The miserable lady with the mean lips and the thin frame sprang out of her seat and grabbed her frayed brown suitcase from overhead. Then she turned her head ever so slightly to the left and muttered "God bless".

"Bye now," I replied. "Have a nice time in Liverpool."

"Huh!" was the extent of her response, offended

no doubt that I had not even enquired about the reason for her visit.

"Let's wait until all these people go," I whispered to my little girl. She was very still now.

I looked out the small window. The sky was grey and threatening, the fields were lush. I sat still on my seat.

"Ruby, we have arrived – we're in Liverpool. Both here for our first time – on a girls' outing in Liverpool – not the type that you would ordinarily choose but, as they say, or as your grandmother would say, 'You have to make the best of a very bad lot'."

I didn't know anything really about the city. I had no connection with it. I had no views on it one way or the other. I was here as a means to an end. It was not the city that perplexed me, but rather the day that lay ahead.

I felt as if was already bedtime. My body was aching and my mind exhausted. The whirlwind tour of my life had left me dog tired . . . and her exhausted or so it seemed. I hoped that she had enjoyed it.

"You can do this, Afric, the worst is over, the waiting is done, just a few more hours and it will be fine. It will be fine, in the end," I whispered to myself.

The plane was almost empty by now. The suits with gadgets stuck to their ears had quickly evacuated the area. Two grey frail-looking ladies, both in wheelchairs, sat there looking vulnerable. I hoped someone kind and gentle would come to get

140

them soon – they looked totally bewildered by all the chaos surrounding them. A mother was wrestling with her son who was howling his head off because he wanted to take the seat belt with him. His frustrated mother was not even bothering to explain why he couldn't. Both he and she were red in the face, him with rage, and her with embarrassment. It was not a good day for them.

My little angel had just woken and I could feel a very faint movement just below my belly button.

"Ruby, time for us two to get moving, to lull you back to sleep. Please don't kick, not today of all days – please, please don't kick your mum any more – it makes me so sad, so sad. Shh, baby, it will all be over soon, very soon, quiet now, go back to sleep for your mummy." I placed my left hand on my rounded stomach. "Shh, my little girl, go back to sleep now."

I stood up and waddled down the narrow aisle of the plane, to the back exit.

In front of me was a beautifully made-up air stewardess. Her eye-shadow was the same two-tone colour as her uniform: matching pale-blue and turquoise-green. Her nails were also two tones: white and pale pink. She looked like a perfect pretty happy little doll. She smiled a mass-produced smile, one that all departing passengers were subjected to. "Have a nice day, now." She rattled it off at me in the same way that they tell you to 'mind the gap,' but really they're not too bothered if you do or if you don't. They were just words without meaning.

I squeezed my eyes tight, very tight, then opened

them and stepped out onto the steps of the plane. I took a deep gulp of Liverpudlian air. My left hand grasped the hand-rail of the steps. I slowly descended onto the tarmac, my right hand caressing my protruding bump. Thankfully she had fallen asleep again. It was only 14:20.

"Ruby, say hello and goodbye to Liverpool," I muttered.

The tide was out on the Mersey, the riverbed was bleak, desolate and lifeless, and it was a dreary drizzly grey day. Apt, I thought, for my angel's second last day on earth.

Chapter 10

A Monday in June, 2013

We walked to the reception of the Foetal Unit Department, Ruby and I. It was not that far – the lady said it was just down the corridor along the cream walls and turn left. She said Jane would be there.

She had big kind welcoming eyes, but they looked just a little bit sad. I wondered was that why they gave her the job, because of her calm dreamy green eyes? She had black curls – they were like perfect springs on a bed, except they had the odd wisp of grey running down them. On the left-hand side of her white tunic was a lopsided gold badge which read '*Jane*'. It felt like weeks since I had talked to her, but in fact it was only two days ago.

"Lynch is the surname, Afric Lynch." Then I offered additional information, I have no idea why. "The address is Apartment 1, Coliemore Road,

Dalkey, County Dublin. I arrived here last night."

"That's great, thank you. Let me have a little look here, darling, to see who you are booked in with."

"Lynch, Lynch, Lynch," she muttered to herself as she scrolled down a long printed paper list. "Of course, I spoke to you on Saturday morning . . . just let me find it here . . . Lynch, oh, here it is. Afric, is that what you said?" Her kind green eyes looked up at me.

"Yes, Afric, Afric Lynch," I replied, having gained a little confidence.

Just then Ruby started moving.

The lady, Jane, had more sense than to tell me I was welcome.

"What a lovely name – Afric. What a beautiful name! It's really a beautiful name," and she repeated it to herself again – "Afric, Afric," – testing how it sounded when she pronounced it.

"Thanks. It's an Irish name, a very old Irish name – it's been in our family for generations." I gently patted my lower tummy in an effort to ease the movement, but the motion got stronger and stronger. My little girl seemed to want to be acknowledged. Fair enough, I thought. It was, after all, her day too.

"Right, let's get you comfortable. You must be tired after the last couple of days. Are you travelling alone?"

"Yes, there's just the two of us, Ruby and me." I paused, not sure if this was the correct answer.

"Oh, another lovely name – though not an Irish one. You know, over the years we've heard so many unusual names that we started keeping a list of the ones we like and, with more and more Irish arriving here every day, the list is getting longer and longer. You know, we joke amongst ourselves that one of these days we'll publish a book with all those great names and it will be a bestseller. Where better to sell the book than right here in one of the largest NHS hospitals in the UK? Ruby is beautiful too – there's a great song by the Beatles – written in the late sixties – that would be well before your time – what's it called? Ruby . . ." Her green eyes fluttered as she struggled to remember it.

"'Ruby Tuesday' is the song," I replied, "but it was a Rolling Stones' song – Mick Jagger sang it."

"That's the one – 'Ruby Tuesday' – how does it go?" Jane had by now abandoned her paperwork.

"God, I don't have a note in my head!" I giggled – but I had a shot at singing a few lines for her.

"That's right, that's the song – it's a great song, isn't it?" She had more sense than to comment on my voice. "Funny that," she continued. "Depending on how the medication goes you might even give birth on Tuesday to your little girl – and we can sing the song together to her." She got up from behind the desk. She was much shorter than I expected her to be.

I smiled gently at her, to thank her for making me feel more at ease.

Jane came around to the front of the desk. She stretched out her arm and pointed to the door. "So, if you want to follow me . . ." She led me to a door which she then opened gently. "This is your consultation room in here."

The room had four chairs and a coffee table. On the wall there was a plastic shelf that held various pamphlets on the NHS.

"It's private, just for you – there won't be any other patients in here. There is a small bathroom just outside the door – next door on the right – and the next door down on the same side is the tea and coffee station – do you see, there to the right? Just help yourself whenever you like. The team that are looking after you will be in very soon to talk to you but, in the meantime, sit down and try to relax." Then she looked me straight in the eyes and said: "Afric, there is nothing to worry about – you are here with us now, the hard bit is over – we will take the very best care of you – there is nothing more to worry about now."

I peered up at her like a lost child who had just been reunited with her mum.

"Are you sure?" I asked.

She sat down beside me and put her wrinkled hand on my left knee. Her hand had small sun spots on it. She wore a simple gold band on her wedding finger. She squeezed my right knee tight.

"Darling, you are in the best place you could possibly be – we do this every day and sometimes three or four times a day. Now you relax and the midwife will be with you soon." She rose and turned on her heel to leave. Then she looked at me once more. "I'll be just in reception – if you need anything just pop out to me." She closed the door behind her.

We were alone, just Ruby and I. We sat down.

The room was small. It was painted cream. They paint walls in hospitals cream and light green because those colours are meant to have a calming effect on patients. The combination of the colours and Jane's green eyes had had a soothing effect on me and Ruby: the kicking had stopped.

There was a large window at the side of the room. It looked out on to the hospital garden. Just below the window was a large rockery, planted with low-size shrubs. All the shrubs in the rockery were different: different shapes and sizes and various shades of green. One of the greens reminded me of my school uniform in secondary school; it was that same bottle green. Green like a Heineken bottle. For years after, I never wore that colour – not because I didn't like school – I couldn't quite figure out why I never wore it – maybe because it reminded me of being institutionalised.

"Now, my little angel, it's going to be time for us to say goodbye very soon. Well, I suppose that it's not really a goodbye, because you will always be with me no matter where I am or what I am doing. My little angel will be with me, but only in spirit. Ruby, you and I are going to do things a little differently: you are going to look after me instead of me looking after you. We're doing it the other way around – arseways, I suppose. I really hope you don't mind taking care of me. I think that it should be pretty low maintenance so it shouldn't take up too much of your time. Though sometimes I lose my temper with your dad because he doesn't listen to me, so maybe you could help me with that, and maybe you could help him to listen. Sometimes I say to him: 'Luke, I don't know why they gave you ears because you never use them.' When I say that it drives him crazy. Do you think that he might react more positively if I said something nice instead of saying something critical? What do you think, Ruby, should I try it? I should, shouldn't I? Can you help me, please, when you're up there?

"You know, driving is another problem – speeding fines – maybe you could help me to slow down just a little bit or maybe I should just buy a slower car – yes, maybe that's a better idea, rather than bothering you with that task – I mean, you already will have lots of people asking you to help them. Yeah, forget that task – I'll get an old crock this time when I get home."

I gazed out the window into the shrubbery. A crisp packet was stuck in between two of the dark-green shrubs. I wondered how many other heartbroken women had sat in this room as their lives changed forever, how many lives were shattered inside these cream walls. I opened the window a little, as the heat in the room was oppressive. I rubbed my stomach in an anti-clockwise direction. The crisp packet fluttered in the warm summer air. I stared blankly at it.

"I hope that you don't think it selfish of me – it seems that I'm getting off easy, doesn't it, not having to care for you or mind you? I won't have to clean any of those stinky nappies or get up in the middle of the night when you're teething. I won't have to worry about rushing you to hospital when you have a fever, and I won't need to worry when you fall over and hurt your head. I won't have to worry – I won't have to worry about anything, only that you are okay wherever you are. I wonder where you'll go? You'll be up in the sky, won't you? Just above my head."

I got up and moved to another cream chair, one that was nearer to the window, where the breeze was refreshing.

"Before we have to say goodbye let's see what one more doctor has to say. This is our last hope, our final chance to maybe save you, Ruby. Do you think that he will tell me that a miracle has occurred and they have found a way to get rid of all the problems with the chromosomes? Maybe they might be able to get the number right – I mean, they only need to count to forty-six – to find forty-six of them and then just make sure that they are arranged okay? Sure it can't be that difficult? Can it? Really? Maybe, Ruby, just maybe. It's worth a try, isn't it? You know, miracles do happen. Maybe because you're so rare you might be a miracle, who knows? You might be a miracle child."

I peered at my rotund stomach; it didn't reply or indicate that it was listening.

"What do you think, Ruby? You tell me: are you meant for this world, or are you destined for a happier place, where you float around all day and check things out? I can imagine you as an angel with beautiful chocolaty eyes like your dad's, and elaborate gilt-edged wings. Will you be that beautiful angel just behind my shoulder? You need to tell me which shoulder you'll be on, so that I know, so that I don't bang you by accident, on a press or something, when I'm in the kitchen."

The crisp packet filled with air. It floated up towards a prickly dark-green bush but got caught on one of the sharp ends of the leaves on the way up. It got stuck. It looked safer there.

"Maybe you'll come back again, only next time your body and soul will both work. We need to get you a proper body, so maybe the next body will be perfect, like all those other tiny bodies in pretty little buggies that other happy mums have, where all the bits are in the right places."

The tears streamed down my face and landed on my swollen belly. There were darker pink patches on my shirt, just above my belly button. It looked as though Ruby had been crying too through my skin and onto my shirt. But the tears were mine, for her.

"Afric, Afric," called a gentle voice.

I looked away from the crisp package to see a low-sized middle-aged lady standing just inside the door. It was Jane.

I had not heard her enter the room. I was so preoccupied that I hadn't heard the door open. I looked from the crisp packet to the shrubbery to her, into her kind eyes.

"Are you okay? Are you ready to see the obstetrician?"

"Sorry, I didn't hear you come in. Yes, I'm ready. I was just telling Ruby what's happening."

Jane's arm was outstretched once again, inviting me to come with her.

The three of us moved, taking those final fatal steps together. No one uttered a word.

The screen was a state-of-the-art fifty-inch TV screen, a kind of a thing that the average Irish male would want for watching sport and mindless thrash like American wrestling. Luke would have loved it. In fact, he would have adored it. It was a screen that took up a lot of the room. This monitor made Mary's one look pathetic.

The room was dark. I would have felt more comfortable if it was a bit brighter.

A medium-sized man, with rimless glasses, a white coat with a silver pen in the top right-hand pocket, stood up when I entered the room. But not to greet me, just to tilt his TV screen so that he didn't have to strain his neck. Then, he moved away from the screen, walked around the examination table and stopped in the middle of the room – as though the centre of the room was neutral ground, safe, away from the scanning equipment and out of range of the intimidating screens.

"I'm Doctor Gimenez. Nice to meet you."

Another 'nice to meet you' person. I wished that I had never met any one of these happy-go-lucky doomsday obstetricians, who seemed to be lining up to greet me with fatal news. I wanted to tell him to piss off. It was not nice to meet him. Not unless he was going to tell me that my child was a miracle, that they had disappeared – all those extra chromosomes. Instead, I told myself to shut up, that I was looking at a last-chance saloon. Give it a chance, I told myself – isn't it worth one last chance?

His eyes didn't seem pleased to meet me. They were devoid of emotion, cold, displaying no sentiment.

"Thank you," I replied. "Thanks for agreeing to see me at such short notice."

He didn't acknowledge my gratitude, barely my presence. He was purely a process man.

The lady with the kind eyes and wrinkled hands motioned for me to lie on the examination table.

He looked only at the screen and seemed to be oblivious to me. This doctor most definitely had not been chosen for his warm bedside manner.

I wanted to ask him was he long at this, looking at babies and delivering tragic news to devastated mothers? I wanted to ask him did he have perfect kids himself? I was intrigued as to why anyone would choose a career where several times day you are faced with telling mothers that their children are incompatible with life. Surely, I thought, no money would pay you for that? Instead, I said nothing.

We were back on telly again, Ruby and I, the Marilyn Monroes of fatal foetal abnormalities. It looked like we too were going to have a tragic end.

He scanned and scanned and scanned. I looked at

his eyes, while he looked at my baby. His eyes gave me no indication of what he saw. He never did look up to meet my gaze; he concentrated only on the screen and on the content of my belly. He didn't speak from the moment that he began to scan.

It felt like an hour as the freezing cold hand-scanner raced up and down and around the bulge in my stomach. He dug hard into my skin, but didn't apologise or acknowledge his investigation.

He finally looked towards the lady with the green eyes and spoke to her over my bump. "I have seen what I need."

The kind lady wiped the slimly gel from my belly and signalled for me to follow her. I did, like a lamb headed for the slaughterhouse. We returned to the room with the cream walls, with the four chairs and a garden window. I sat down and she went out, closing the door from the outside.

Ruby and I were alone once again. I walked to the window because I needed to do something, anything. I looked for the crisp packet and stared and stared at it.

There was no miracle, there was no happy ending to the series, and it was not the movies. My tiny angel was incompatible with life. This was the end. But, it would all be fine, in the end.

There was a knock on the door and Jane entered, ushering in the man with the rimless glasses and the white coat. They sat down, facing me.

It took him only seconds to confirm that the original prognosis was correct. It was Patau

Syndrome with all the complications associated with that fatal foetal syndrome. He listed them all. The list was long and definitely longer than two days earlier in Dublin. Things, it seemed, were not getting any better. Instead the complications were growing. He said that the results of the amniocentesis had arrived first thing from Glasgow – they confirmed what he had seen on the screen – Patau Syndrome.

"When you are ready, we will proceed."

His eyes didn't meet mine; they looked above my head, as though he was looking at the back of my head, but from the front, like I myself had learned to do with people. Nor did he use my name or my little girl's name – he didn't even have the courtesy to ask what her name was – how bloody rude, I thought. I considered for a second introducing them but decided against it.

His job was the procedure and that was where it began and ended. We were the next procedure.

"Thank you." I looked at Jane and then at the man with the rimless glasses and white coat. "If we can please have just a minute – so I can explain what is wrong to my little girl?" As I spoke my voice began to quiver.

Doctor Gimenez slowly got up and left the room. He didn't utter a word, nor did he glance back. Instead he firmly closed the door, shutting out any emotions. Jane patted my hand and then followed him.

"You see, Ruby, what happened was that when we were making you we got it wrong. Making a person is like building a house with Lego. All the blocks have got to go into the right places. Chromosomes are like the Lego blocks – they are the blocks that make up a person. And if the Lego blocks aren't in right place then the house will fall down. The same kind of thing happens with a person if the chromosomes aren't right. Do you understand what I'm trying to tell you? Think of it this way: if you're baking a cake and add too much flour and don't put in enough eggs, then the cake won't rise, it will stay flat. That is because you don't have the correct ingredients, and it is the same with a person. All the ingredients need to be right for a person to be compatible with life.

"You see, what happened is that we made a mistake. Not just a small one; we made a big mistake, a fatal mistake. We gave you too many chromosomes, far too many. When someone is being created each cell in your body is meant to have two copies of chromosomes. But, when your dad and I were making you, we got it wrong, so very wrong, so in lots of the cells in your tiny body you have three copies of chromosome 13 instead of two. This means you have a disorder called trisomy 13 – it's also called Patau Syndrome. That is what has made you so sick, what has made you incompatible with life.

"But we didn't know – we had no idea that we had created an imperfect being. I am so sorry, Ruby. Your dad doesn't know yet, he doesn't know anything about the whole chromosome business. I think that we'll keep it as just our secret, a girls' secret. I think it would make him very sad if he knew about it. I would be afraid, Ruby, that he might never stop being sad ever, and if he got that sad maybe he would never be happy again and then it would be like having lost two people." I stood by the window, gulping in Liverpudlian air, in an attempt to calm myself. "You see, I could lose him because he doesn't have the tools to cope with sadness. For me, when you're gone, I'll suffer from a huge dollop of old-fashioned painful heartache, but eventually that heartbreak will fade. That doesn't mean that I will ever forget you – it will simply mean that instead of thinking of you all the time, I will think of you only a few times a day. Luke is different – his sadness is much deeper, it eats at his mind and spreads to every cell in his body, like a disease. Because he doesn't know how to mourn, it will make him dreadfully sad, and that sadness is like being alive but not present in the world."

I sat down: my feet were tired from carrying my precious cargo.

"Patau Syndrome – it's a funny-sounding name, isn't it? – it's called after the man that discovered it. He was from Germany. This condition makes you so unique that if you lived you would be only one in ten thousand who have this disorder. But the chances of your living are so tiny, that even if you were born alive, there is an ninety-per-cent chance you would die in the first year. You would die because your tiny little deformed body is incompatible with life. Fate has decided that you are not meant to be alive.

Imagine, Ruby, being that rare, that unique. For every ten thousand people born there is only one like you. You are so rare that we should put you in a museum. If you were a painting we would hang you in a gallery, with a bronze nameplate explaining why you are so exclusive. It would tell people all about chromosome thirteen. It might even say that thirteen is considered an unlucky number by many people. Then people would pay to come and see you, like they used to pay to go and see freaks in a circus. You see, my little angel, with trisomy 13 your brain has not developed at all."

Ruby began to move ever so slightly, as if acknowledging she had heard my explanation. Her movement felt like popcorn exploding under my skin, just below my belly button – just as Luke had said.

"The doctor already told me that your feet aren't working either. Did I tell you this already? And they are pretty sure that there is a big hole at the bottom of your back, and you see it is not that easy to make your back better. Ruby, they can't fix your body, it is just too sick. If there was just one or two things wrong then maybe but because all the cells have been made incorrectly, they can't help us, Ruby. You are too sick to live. So you see we didn't make you perfect like other babies, we made you imperfect. So, your body and its organs don't work properly, and some of them don't even exist. You are really screwed up. The consultant, he said that someone has to be that statistic. Do you know what they say, that tough times are sent to people to make them stronger? So, my sweetheart, you are the one. You were chosen to be the tough one and by God you are that, my Teflon angel, hanging on with all your might, your mighty heart defying nature and keeping you alive. They say what doesn't kill you will make you stronger. So I suppose in this instance the cliché is a double header: it will kill you and make me stronger.

"Just now, in a minute – it is time for us to say goodbye, our last goodbye. You are not to worry about anything – I promise you won't feel a thing. I know that you can't feel a thing – they told me that you won't know what is happening. Ruby, it would be so cruel for me to bring you into the world when you don't have a brain – you could never do anything for yourself. You could never have your own thoughts. You would never have your very own wishes and dreams. There would be no colour in your world – your life would be like mine now, an old fuzzy black-and-white TV. You would have to live your life through us, and that would be so terribly selfish and cruel of us. You would never get drunk, fall in love, laugh with friends or swim in the sea. Life, Ruby, can be so very cruel, but I do not want it to be cruel to you, so you have to go somewhere else, my tiny little angel, you have to go to another place where it is not cruel, where people are kind. Do you see up there in the clouds, where you just float around, hang out and eat sweets all day and check out all the humans that you have to look after? That's a much nicer life, what do you think?"

"Do you remember when we went on the whirlwind tour of my life, just yesterday morning in Dublin? Do you remember that we visited two people's houses – Henry's and Penny's? One house was next door to the pub, with the black door, where Penny lived, the lady with the coloured dresses, do you remember? And then we went to the dusty pink house with the blue door and the flowers outside where Henry lived. Well, Ruby, when you go from here today, they will be waiting for you. Henry and Penny will be waiting for you. They will take you by your little hands to some place where you'll be happy. They are good kind people; they will love and mind you. They, my little angel, will be your parents until I get there. You are to be a good girl and do what they say – be good until I get there. And remember what your grandmother used to say: mind your manners, and always say please and thank you. Because you are with them and not with us doesn't mean your mummy and daddy don't love you any less – it's just that we cannot be with you just yet. Later we will, I promise – much later, we will come to you. We really love you, and that is why I am saying goodbye to you today, before your time. You see, today, Ruby, you will be born asleep, with your tiny little eyes closed – that is, of course, if we bothered to give you any eyes – I hope that we got that bit right, I hope that we gave you eyes, two of them . . . I wonder what colour your eyes are? I wonder would you be right or left-handed? I hope we gave you hands – I don't want to see my baby without hands – please let us have given you hands, two hands with ten fingers. Is that too much to ask? I would like you to be okay on the outside – it's okay if you're totally screwed up on the inside because I can't see that."

Jane opened the door. "Whenever you're ready, Afric."

I rubbed my bump one last time. "Bye, my tiny baby . . . I love you, Ruby, and your dad does too – he just could not be here today, it would have made him too sad. We love you, my little angel, we will love you forever. Now go to them – they are waiting for you – he and she are waiting with their arms out to collect you – go now and don't keep them waiting any longer. And be good for Mummy, be the best girl until I come to get you."

Jane handed me two blue pills that would induce me. I swallowed them.

Ruby lay still inside my stomach.

Chapter 11

A Tuesday in June, 2013

Early Tuesday morning Ruby was delivered with the same care, dedication and dignity as all other babies – nothing different – except she was perfectly still when she came into the world. The lady with the kind face greeted her – she called her by her name – I was happy she did that.

They took her away and then she arrived into my room in a glass box with a lid and shiny chrome wheels under it.

She was pushed by a midwife with another kind round face. The person pushing the box wore a white outfit. On the right-hand side of her tunic, she wore a gold name-badge. It read '*Lucy*' in dark brown lettering. Her badge was not lopsided like Jane's.

They keep a famous mummy called Juanita in a glass box just like it in Peru. I have visited it. The girl in the box in Peru is over ten thousand years old. The girl in this box was minus three months old. Neither age seemed to make sense. I thought the box and its contents should be in that museum and not a foetal abnormalities unit in a hospital.

I thought it only polite to get up to greet my daughter – after all, that is what you normally do when you meet someone for the first time, isn't it, and I hadn't really seen her when she was delivered.

I moved myself to the edge of the bed and carefully placed my two feet firmly on the wooden floor. I stood up straight, very straight. I walked past the wardrobe on my left and arrived at the middle of the room. There I stood facing the door and the box. I had been alone in the room for a while. I was glad to have company.

The box approached nearer to me. I didn't move, I didn't take a single step. The prospect of meeting my own deformed flesh and blood utterly terrified me. I was frozen, like that mummy in Peru. I didn't budge an inch from the middle of the maternity suite with the cream walls.

I hoped that my little angel didn't think me rude, not rushing to greet her. I stared at the box, and stared and stared.

Her words called me back to reality. She called my name gently – no, not the girl in the box, the lady pushing the box, the lady in the white tunic.

"Afric, this is your daughter, your tiny little angel, Ruby."

The lady with the round face parked the box like you might park a car, some feet away from me. There was me, the bed with tubes attached, the wardrobe and now the box; the room was far too big for so few things.

It was a kind of standoff. She was there, I was here and we had to meet in the middle. Except she was in the box and I wasn't, so I had to do all the hard yards.

The box twinkled in the warm June sunshine; different colours of the rainbow danced on the top of the glass container. The colours were beautiful. At least she had got sunshine for her only day on earth. I thought it pretty decent of them to give us a good day for our meeting – well, seeing as how we had got everything else so wrong, that was the least that could be done – send us a couple of rays for our get-together. It was good to have something to talk about – after all, isn't that what Irish people talk about mostly – the weather?

I stood there frozen, glaring at the container, watching the sun dance on my little girl. I was terrified of what I might see. What if I didn't like what I saw? Would that mean that she would think that I didn't love her? Would she know and then be awfully offended? I didn't want to upset her on her only day on earth.

Obviously, I had not planned her day that well if she was going to spend it in a box. She could not spend all day in a box on her own – sure she would be bored stupid. I wondered if Lucy had put a toy in the box to keep her company. It must be so lonely all on her own with no one to talk to or nothing to play with. Nothing to do, just lie there and be dead. To be born asleep for your only day on earth would be pretty uninteresting for Ruby, I thought.

Maybe I should take her for a walk, a walk in the Liverpool sunshine. But where would I take her? Would we both end up lost because I didn't know this city at all?

Maybe if the box's wheels were sturdy enough I could take her to the garden? I could take her to the shrubbery just outside the window, the bushes with all the different green-coloured plants – I could show her the green of my school uniform. I could show her the crisp packet stuck in the bush. This room had cream walls too and a window, but it did not look out onto the shrubbery like the first room. I was not sure that I would be able to find the rockery with the crisp packet and what if we managed to find the shrubbery but the crisp packet had flown away, and then she might be very disappointed?

The lady stood still in the middle of the room, in a white uniform, with the box. She didn't move. The box had not moved any closer to me, nor I to it. The sunlight still danced on its lid, as though the light was trying to tempt me towards it.

"I have washed and dressed Ruby, Afric," said the lady. "I will leave her here with you, so that you can spend some time together. Just buzz me when you're ready and I will come and collect her. You can have as much time as you like together." Slowly she walked towards the cream door. She turned as she was halfway out the door and said: "I've taken some photos of her for you to take home with you."

"You're so kind. Thank you so much, Lucy."

She smiled. "Call me if you need me."

"I will. Thank you, Lucy."

Now it was just me and her alone, with her in a box. How were we going to fill the time? It wasn't like we could play a game, or I could throw a ball and she could chase it. You see, when Ruby was in my stomach it was on my terms and conditions – she had to stay there and I couldn't see her – so, I guess in lots of ways it was not reality. Now was reality. A reality that I had not wished for.

I was terrified that she would look all mixed up, with all the bits in the wrong places. I stood in the middle of a large cream room with a glass box that contained my daughter. I stood there for a while, letting the shock register that there in the glass box was my little angel. She would never walk, run, swim or play with me – her tiny little confused body prevented that. This world was not the place for her body. Maybe her soul could be here but not her body.

I took a few steps towards the box and stopped a few more short of it. From a distance I peered into it, hoping to see from where I stood how bad things were inside the box.

The person in the box wore a blue outfit. A babygro with an elephant on it in a deeper blue colour and small white buttons running down the front. Her eyes were closed, so I didn't know if they were dark chocolate-brown, hazel-green or they might even have been blue, steel-blue. I will never know. I didn't think to ask the lady with the round face. I forgot to ask. How I could have been so stupid as to forget something as important as that? I wonder did the lady know? I wonder did we remember to give her eyes at all?

On a fluffy off-white blanket lay a tiny body wearing a blue babygro and a blue hat. Things seemed relatively normal at a first glance. She didn't look like a deformed monster, which had been my biggest fear. What if she looked like a freak and I was terrified of her? What if her abnormalities scared me? Wouldn't it be awful to be terrified of your own flesh and blood, to be terrified of something that you created? Scared of someone that we had fucked up so badly? Wouldn't it be sad to judge your own daughter by what she looked like and even worse to be scared of her because of her imperfect features?

I bent over to be a bit closer, yet far enough away to keep my distance. Then I took the three scariest steps of my life.

I arrived at the box.

My phone blipped and blipped again. I looked back at the bedside locker where it vibrated furiously. I let it ring out. I could answer it later.

I was finally going to meet my daughter for the first time, in fact the only time, ever. *Afric Meets Ruby* sounds like a movie, doesn't it? Whatever about it being a tragedy, I desperately hoped it would not be a horror show.

I stood over the box and peered into it – into it at her, below. There she was in the sparkling clear box.

Ruby had the body and face of a baby that was just a little too tiny for this world. She was tiny, so very tiny. But perfect, my little angel was perfect. She lay there asleep, asleep forever, she would never be awake. I can't describe the relief of seeing her appear normal – she looked like an undersized normal baby at a glance. I was not terrified or horrified by my tiny girl; it was a feeling of relief. My tiny angel looked like a baby and not a gremlin.

I opened the lid on the box as you might open the top of a fish tank. I looked down on her lying there on the fluffy white blanket. I bent over her and scooped her up into my arms. I was holding my own flesh and blood, Ruby Lynch, in my arms. She lay there lifeless and almost weightless.

While I held her, I waited and waited, not sure what I was waiting for, and maybe I expected her to wake up, to cry out loud. She lay in my arms motionless. She weighted the same amount as a half pound of butter.

The outfit was far too big for her, especially the matching blue hat. Ruby only needed a very tiny hat, because she didn't have any back to her head. It was missing – we had forgotten to include it – another bloody mistake. She had a front to her head but no back. Or so the kind woman with the round face told me afterwards. The nurse said she looked just like me. I wasn't sure if that was a good or bad thing, to have your deformed baby looking like you, but I thanked her anyway.

"Ruby, we made another mistake when we made

you – we gave you six fingers on your left hand instead of five. We got your feet wrong too because they're twisted inwards so that they look like they're looking at each other. Couldn't we get anything right? God, Ruby, your parents are a disaster – we made you all wrong – oh, my little angel! We are so sorry for making such a mess of you."

Of course, we had forgotten to finish her back too. We never bothered to fuse her spine, so there was a large hole at the bottom of her back. She was like a job that was only half-done on the outside. The inside was not much better, I later learnt – we got all the organs wrong too. Some were too big, others too small, bits that were meant to meet other bits didn't. Other bits that were not meant to meet ever had been stuck together. We had made a mess of our little angel.

My fingers touched the side of her cheek. Her skin was soft and perfectly tender like a normal baby's skin, but it was very purply-pink – it was the wrong colour, but that was because we had not finished making her before she went to sleep. She smelt like a baby, she looked like a baby, but she was a dead baby. I held her and hoped that she would move, that she would come back to life but she remained motionless in my arms.

"Ruby, I am just going to go to the wardrobe for a second. I am going to get a photo to show you – a photo of our wedding day."

Should I take her with me, I thought. I meant, to the wardrobe? It was very near.

I raised her up in my arms so her tiny tiny face was closer to me. I looked at her closed eyes and whispered, "Do you want to come with me to the wardrobe – see it just there – the brown one? I mean, it would be somewhere to go – something to do – do you want to come or would you prefer to stay on the bed? The only thing is you will be alone on the bed and you might fall off. What do you think, Ruby? Will we go to the wardrobe – you and I – take a stroll?"

So, I took her for a walk, to the wardrobe. She didn't seem to mind. I opened the brown doors and reached inside. I pulled out a brown envelope with my left hand while I cradled her carefully in my right arm. I retraced my steps and sat down on the bed. I put Ruby on the bed, just next to me, while I opened the envelope.

Ruby and the A4 envelope were pretty similar in length – they both looked lost on the big bed with all the tubes.

"Ruby, stay as you are – you are not to move – stay right there – be careful and don't roll off the edge of the bed. I don't want you to fall. You might hurt yourself and we don't want that now."

But what would it matter if she fell and bounced her head off the floor? It didn't matter because there was only her face to hurt – she could not bump the back of her head because she had no back to her head, and anyway she couldn't feel it. Nevertheless, I didn't want her to roll off the edge. The lady with the kind eyes would think me a terrible person if she fell and I would not like her to think that I was a bad mother. After all, it was only a few hours that I had to look after my tiny angel.

I opened the envelope and pulled out the black-and-white picture with the one hundred and fifty people.

"Look, Angel, there are Henry and Penny. Do you see them there in the picture, sitting down in the foreground? Look – do you see them? Please tell me that your tiny little soul is with them. Tell me that it is only your messed-up little body that is here with me. Please, tiny angel, send me a sign to tell me you are happy with them."

But she appeared uninterested, so I brought the picture closer so that she could see it better. Of course I had forgotten, distracted by the outing to the wardrobe. It was not that she wasn't interested – it was simply that her eyes were closed. The nurse with the kind eyes had closed her eyes because she was asleep forever.

I looked down at her. "Ruby, I know that your dad and I would not forget to give you eyes – of course we gave you eyes so you could see a few colours – but don't worry, my little girl – if you can't see the photo, I will tell you about the people in it."

I looked at her head underneath the ridiculously enormous hat. I could see there were two little ears, one on each side of her head.

"Thank God for that, Ruby – we got one thing right – we managed to give you two ears and they are even in the right place." I kissed her perfect ears on each side of her head. I rubbed them with my middle and index fingers, very gently, as if congratulating them for being there at all. Or maybe I was praising myself, or applauding us as a couple for getting one thing right.

"The photo, Ruby, was taken two years ago – oh, there's the phone bleeping – I bet that was your dad – I'll call him back in a minute. That was our wedding day in the picture – it was the longest happiest day of my life – isn't it very cruel for you to be born on the same day you died? Your birthday and anniversary the same day – I mean, that is kind of happy and sad, isn't it? Everything on the same day – a very busy day.

"Do you see that guy, standing there beside your mum? Yes, him there, that is your dad – that is Luke – can you see him? He's handsome, isn't he? You know, when I first met him, I used to tell him that he had eyes like Dairy Milk Chocolate – there was an ad on the telly once for Cadbury's Dairy Milk Chocolate where the dark chocolate swirled around and around white chocolate and his eyes reminded me of that ad. When I first met your dad, I would get lost in those eyes, I could gaze at them forever. I have not done that for so long – I wonder why?"

I moved my daughter closer to my chest, but she didn't notice, she didn't respond. I lowered my head and kissed my little girl on the top of her nose. Maybe because we got it right: it was there in the right place.

"There, Ruby, that is from your dad." I clutched

her closer to my chest. "And that is a hug from your dad." Her body remained motionless. It was soft. I didn't grasp her too tight for fear of breaking her underdeveloped bones. "He gives the best hugs. I used to call them bone-crushers before we got married when he would come at weekends to visit me in my tiny cottage. When he arrived at Dublin Airport, he would drop his bag, right there on the floor in the middle of the arrivals hall and give me the biggest hug – so tight that it would hurt your bones. This time when he comes back, I am going to give him a bone-crusher. I think that we will need it, Ruby. I think that I will need the biggest hug of my life when I get home.

"Can you see all the freckles that your dad has in that photo? Look, there on his nose, just there – see all his stuck-together freckles? You see what happens is when sun comes out during the summer it makes the freckles seem alive, like they are singing and dancing on your dad's face. His face gets very busy then with all the freckles – he even gets them on his lips – look at the photo – it looks like he's eating them. Do you think it looks like that? By the end of the summer there are so many of them that there is not enough room for each individual one. So then they all merge and then it looks like he has funny-shaped islands all over his face. One year we played a game, to see how many freckle islands we could name. I found an island on his right cheek that was the shape of Koh Samui in Thailand. Your dad and I went there once a long time ago – that was how we knew its shape. Then in winter the freckles are different – they are like they are uncared-for, like they are lonely – isolated – in winter there are no islands on his face."

The door opened very gently and a hand with sunspots and a thin gold band appeared on the inside of it. Jane stepped into the room. She walked ever so slowly in the direction of the bed.

"Good morning, Afric," she said in a gentle tone. "How are you doing, my dear? May I have a little look at Ruby – at your little girl?" Slowly she approached. She walked past the empty glass container, past the wardrobe, and arrived at the side of the bed with the brown covers.

"Hi, Jane – I'm glad you came – I was hoping that you were working today – I wanted you to meet my little girl." Then I announced proudly: "Ruby, this is Jane – Jane, this is Ruby."

Jane looked intently at her. "She looks okay, doesn't she?"

"I think that she looks fine – when she's all dressed up you would never know how sick she was," I responded.

"Of course you wouldn't. The name . . ." she paused, "the name Ruby really suits her – I think it's a good choice."

"Glad that you like it," I answered. I hoped that she wasn't saying that her name matched the colour of my little girl's face – I thought it best not to comment anyway. Jane was a kind person – she would not think like that.

"Afric, I got the lyrics of the song – her song – I have them here – do you want them? Shall we sing her song to her?" Her hand, the one with the band, was outstretched as she offered me the paper.

But I could not take it because I had my hands full.

"That would be lovely, yes, please, Jane – but, if you would sing, we will listen – is that okay?" I wasn't sure if that was the response she wanted.

The lady with the perfect black curls and the green dreamy eyes came and sat next to Ruby and me on the bed – she placed her hand on my arm and she sang Ruby's song to us . . . "Goodbye, Ruby Tuesday" . . .

When she finished Ruby and I stood up – we gave her a standing ovation but without the clapping. Jane seemed happy with us – and Ruby seemed to like her song too. It was nice for her to have some music for her only day on earth and we had managed to give her ears too – so it was good she got to use them.

Jane's kind eyes looked across the bed at me. "Can I get you anything, Afric? Would you like a cup of tea or coffee?"

I looked from the blue bundle of death in my arms, into her caring eyes. "I would love a cup of tea, please, with just one sugar, thanks for asking – but Ruby won't have anything – she's fine."

She smiled gently at me. "You two seem to be getting on well. Take as long as you like – you can have all the time in the world."

But we didn't have all the time in the world: we had just some hours to connect.

174

The door closed gently behind Jane.

I could feel my eyes quiver – they started to feel like they were a size too big for my eye-sockets. I looked directly ahead of me and gently began to sob. The tears rolled down my cheeks and stained her tiny blue outfit. The tear stains looked huge on the miniature clothes. I had ruined her outfit on her only day on earth – how selfish, I thought. Maybe I should ask the nurse if we should change her outfit. I was afraid that she might get cold. But of course she would not feel it; she would never feel what it is like to get cold.

"Your dad has sticky-up hair. It stands up at the back of his head near his crown – it drives him nuts when it's upright like a poker. I told him once that he should use a hair-straightener – he didn't think that funny so now we never talk about it – now if he asks is it okay, I always say yes. Before, when things were different, very different, when we used to laugh out loud a lot, I would lick my hand and pat his hair down for him – but he doesn't like me doing that any more, so it just sticks up all the time and we both pretend it's okay. I often wonder if other people notice.

"These days, Ruby, we pretend lots of things are okay but we both know they are not. Pretending is often easier than talking, so we pretend, though this time, I think, the pretending game is over. We are going to have to talk about things – we are going to have to talk about you. What am I going to tell him, what am I going to say, how will I explain to him what happened, what happened to you, why you were so fatally flawed?

"You see, there are a few reasons why I didn't bring him along today. The main one is because I am afraid he will get very very sad and stay sad forever. But another reason is because he is a perfectionist. Do you know what that means? Do you know what a perfectionist is? Well, what it means is that everything that your dad does has to be done one-hundred-per-cent correct and right. He would not understand why you are not perfect. He fears imperfection, and it terrifies him. The thought of you, albeit a perfect you, makes him very happy. I hope you don't think me selfish but it would be very hard for me now to have lost you and then to lose your dad again to that kind of sorrow. I hope that makes sense to you. Do you understand now why I decided not to bring him along? He would want something perfect and you are imperfect in every way. It would have been a disaster for all of us. Anyway, he might say the wrong thing to you and I didn't want him to upset you on your birthday."

Chapter 12

Jane came in and placed a black cup of hot liquid on the bedside locker. She smiled at me and then gave a second smile to Ruby. She didn't utter a word and then she left the room.

She closed the door very gently behind her. We were alone again.

I picked up the black-and-white photo, as if to reignite Ruby's interest or maybe to just pass the time.

"I wonder, Ruby, would you have been like your dad or your mum? Would you have been calm, methodical, persistent and a perfectionist like him, or would you have been outgoing, outrageous and bubbly like me? What do you think? Who would you be like? Maybe you would not be like either of us – instead just your own person, totally different to both of us.

"But the reality is that you got the worst of both of us. Your mum and dad fucked you up. It seems that you brought out the worst in us both – our fault – and then you ended up like this, because of us."

I placed my little girl back on the white blanket. It was easier to talk to her when I could look directly at her face. I wanted to remember exactly what her face was like. I wanted it etched in my memory forever. I wanted to be able to recall every tiny detail. I didn't have much time to record in my mind her every feature. Of course the nurse had taken photos for me – but that was not the same as imprinting her image on my mind.

I looked at every inch of her from the very top of her deformed head right down to the tips of her toes.

We had got her feet wrong, but I had to know about her toes. Had we given her the correct number of toes? Had we remembered to give her any toes?

I lifted up her left leg – very gently – I was afraid of damaging her little bones. Slowly, very slowly, I opened the button on the babygro nearest to her ankle, from her ankle I would peer down the babygro – I would have a kind of preliminary look – I would have a quick look to see what the story was – at the end of the foot.

I took a deep breath and glanced down – quickly – inside the cloth – then I looked away again very quickly. Yes, I had seen some toes – there were definitely toes down there. The next job was to count them – I don't know why but I desperately more than anything wanted her to have ten toes.

I don't know how but miraculously each of her wonky feet had five perfect toes, surprisingly all in the correct order and even the right size. I smiled – delighted with my discovery – I was relieved, so relieved – so I kissed each one of her ten toes – for just being there. I wondered how we got some bits, like her toes, perfect and other bits that would seem easier to make, all wrong.

"Ruby, we don't have a long time so I need to tell you about the rest of the family, the family that are on this earth, because you hopefully won't get to meet them for a while. You will only meet Henry and Penny – your soul is probably with them now, and your petite body is with me for just a while, on a temporary loan.

"If you look to the left, the far left of the photo, do you see the lady with the pink silk suit, the tall lady with the long nose? That is your grandmother. Her name is Elizabeth but we call her Lizzy. Elizabeth is too formal and doesn't suit her because she is full of fun and love. 'Lizzy' describes her better. I told her about you, I told her that you weren't perfect. She knows and she doesn't mind. She still loves you, and she wanted to come here today for your birthday. She said she would be very happy to fly from Dublin to meet you but I thought it better for it just to be you and me and no one else."

The lunch-time summer sunlight invaded the room. I moved the glass box a little to the left so that it was back in the sunshine once more. From the bed Ruby and I watched it twinkle in the summer sunlight.

"Ruby, your mum is just like the Arctic Tern I told you about – chasing the sunshine around the room.

"You would have loved Lizzy, Ruby. She would have dressed you up in funky cool clothes – she would not have allowed frilly girly numbers. She would have taught you lots of things. She would have taught you to be kind to old people, to help them across the road, to carry their shopping. She would have taught you not to judge people because of their looks or their disabilities. Lizzy is full of common sense and most of all she would have taught you how to be positive about everything, how to make the best out of a bad situation. Your situation would be a challenge, even for her. So when I told her about spending the day with you, she told me to enjoy it, that it would be one of the most important days of my life, that even if I was a mother for only one day, to enjoy it, to remember and relish it. You see, Lizzy won't ask what was wrong with you – she is not that kind of person – instead she will ask what was right with you. Now we know that conversation won't take long, will it? She will understand and move on to something else – that is what she is like. She is positive and kind, two very important traits in life.

"Maybe you would have been like her. She's a bit of a legend. I think that you are just like her – you are a fighter too. With all the abnormalities you should have died weeks or months ago, but no, you held on in there. You are a Teflon baby – you stuck with me. It was your mighty racing heart that kept you alive – when nothing much else was working properly, your heart kept everything going. But now that mighty heart of yours has stopped. You can rest now, Ruby, you don't need to fight any more. You have lost the fight and now it is time to rest in peace, to be at peace. Your body has done its bit – now it is time for your soul to take over.

"You see, what happened was that they only gave you on loan to me for just one day – today – isn't one day very short – much too short? And now you have to go elsewhere, where you are better off. They're just teasing me by giving you to me for just a day. Ruby, life can be very cruel sometimes. They will never know how sad it makes me that you're all messed up, they will never understand the pain of holding your dead baby. Do you know what it feels like, my little angel? It is like being physically torn apart from the inside out, piece by piece. It feels as though there is now a huge hole in my heart that will never be filled.

"Ruby, I must stop being so selfish, making you sad on your birthday. I never even got you a present, or a card, and I forgot to get a little cake with candles. How many candles would you put on a dead baby's birthday cake? I suppose I could have just put a plastic nought, a single nought, because in reality you are in minus figures, you are minus three months. I should have bought a thirty-one cake decoration and lie the number one down horizontally beside the three. That would make it a minus-three-months birthday cake. That would be

181

your exact age. Why did I not think of that? God, the least that I could have arranged on your birthday was a cake with candles.

"At least I will have photos of your birthday. The nice nurse with the kind eyes told me she has taken some pictures of you – she took them just before we met, you and I, before she wheeled you in. I wonder did she use the red-eye reduction? Not for your eyes, Ruby, but for your whole body. You are very reddy-pink – you look like you've been badly sunburnt, and you have a kind of red glow off you. The nurse told me the reason you're a funny colour is because your skin at only six months has not fully formed – that is why you're so blotchy – but in the photos you will be all dressed up in your blue outfit and they won't be able to see your skin, only your face. Your blue hat covers the top of your head, so it is only your perfect pretty little face that they will be able to see."

My phone vibrated on the bedside locker. I left my baby alone in the glass box and walked from the centre of the room over to the side of the bed. My phone continued to chime.

"Ruby, it's your dad again, calling to check in on his girls."

Then I turned my back on the glass box. I had to shut out the box and its contents for just a few moments. I sat on the bed, where just over three hours earlier I had given birth to a dead baby. I stared at the head of the bed, at the clear tubes that had drugged me – those tubes with the liquid that had tried to numb the pain.

"Now, Ruby, not a word while I speak to your dad." I touched my lips lightly with my left index figure, to indicate for my daughter to be silent.

"Hi, Luke, lovely to hear from you," I chirped down the phone.

"You too, Afric, babes. I was trying to get you earlier, about an hour ago. Did you see a missed call from me? Is everything okay with you? Are you okay?" He seemed concerned.

I hesitated. "I'm grand – at this bloody IT conference – sorry I couldn't answer earlier – we were in the middle of a presentation. We're on a coffee break now – so it's good you called."

"How are you feeling, Afric? Are you tired from all the travelling?"

Jaysus, if only he knew – the bloody travelling was only half the battle. No, darling, I wanted to respond, I am fucked from giving birth to your dead daughter.

"Yes, I am a little tired but that is to be expected. I'll get a good night's sleep tonight and then tomorrow I'll be grand." The tears began to well up in my eyes, and I dug my fingernails into my palm so very hard this time that I was afraid they might pierce the skin and draw blood.

"Afric, Afric?" The pitch of his voice increased slightly the second time he said my name. "Afric, sweetheart, can you hear me?"

I glared at the tubes, and swallowed hard. "How is China, how is work going?" I was desperately trying to change the direction of the conversation, to get him to talk.

"Oh fine – you know, dealing with difficult rich Chinese clients with no morals – dangerous people to be negotiating with. Actually, truthfully, it is pretty awful. I really miss you in every sense. Honestly, I'm not sure how much longer I can do this – this life – you know it is no life. My life has become airports, hotels, business meetings, impossible wealthy clients. My life is passing me by, and our lives are passing us by."

I turned and looked at the glass box. It had not moved and she had not stirred, not an inch. She was just a fraction outside the range of the sunlight, so I went and gently moved her a few inches to the right so that she would once again enjoy the glow of the midday sun.

Luke sounded pretty low, though calm. An unusual combination, I thought.

I really don't need this now, I thought. A dead baby and a husband having grim dark feelings. Christ, this man can pick his moments. "Really, Luke, what makes you say that?" I focused my gaze again on the clear tubes to the left of the bed. I concentrated on steadying my voice. I must let him do the talking and me the listening.

"You know, since the scan I have been so excited, so excited about us having a baby together, about the three of us being a family. Maybe it has made me reprioritise my life, our life together. I don't want the life that I have at the moment. I have given my life to this job. We don't swim together any more or hang out together – all those fun times seem to have stopped. And I was just thinking today all we're doing as a couple is going through the motions of living, but it is not much of a life, is it? Afric, we used to be so close and now we have drifted apart, and now I realise it is my fault. It is entirely my fault because I wanted the dream home, the expensive car and nice life style. But not any more, Afric. I would rather live in the upstairs apartment with the shabby stairs with its bright yellow door. I just want to come home now to you, to you and our baby, for it to be like it was before, way back, when we were hopelessly in love, kissing in the sea, blowing bubbles underneath the water."

Now he didn't seem down, just sure about what he wanted the future to hold for the three of us. When those dreams were crushed what would happen then? It could be the beginning of one his deep sadnesses.

I sat down on the bed, still with my back to the glass box. I continued to glare at the clear tubes; they helped me focus on keeping it together.

"Luke, I miss you too, I miss you so much. I wish you were with me right now, I wish you were beside me, holding my hand." My voice began to quiver. It was okay, it was safe to cry now. I could cry and he would think that it was our conversation that had me in tears. I shut Ruby out from the conversation; I focused on talking to Luke. He would just think that it was those blasted hormones again. And, by God, was he right! Those hormones were racing uncontrollably through my veins.

Luke cleared his throat. He lowered his voice – not the low pitch he uses when he is sad but instead the calm tone that he uses when he wants me to listen, to concentrate on what he is saying. "I need to tell you something. A few weeks back I applied for a position internally in Sheppard Consulting, a different role, a management role. I have already done two interviews and it's down to the last three candidates. The final interview is next week, next Tuesday. I didn't want to tell you in case I don't get the job, but they emailed me today to ensure that I would take the position if it was offered to me. I suppose they don't want to look stupid offering it to me, for me to then say no. It would mean no more long hours travelling, no more endless days away from you. It would give the three of us an opportunity to be together as a family. I thought it would be a good idea to chat to you before I responded to their email. What do you think, Afric? If they offer me the position should I take it for us? So that we get another chance at being happy?"

"Yes, Luke, we need to change some things in our life, we need to go back to being happy – when it was just you and me and we were blissfully happy. If you think that it is time to give up working in China – to come home – then yes – yes, I think you should take the position – but it needs to be something that you want. If it is what you really want then say yes . . . but you know sometimes things are not what we expect – they turn out to be different, very different . . . but, if you're happy to be home, say yes – say yes, you will take the position, and we can start again – try again – go back to the beginning."

"Afric, I have decided that even if I don't get the promotion I am quitting. I am calling it a day. I am not breaking my balls for some international consultancy firm, making them rich. It is going to be on my terms from now on. For the past eighteen months, I have worked and travelled day and night. We have had to put our relationship on hold while I flitted around the world, and I am done with it now. It is our time now to really become a family."

He paused after his oration – was he waiting for me to respond? Or was he ready for the off again? Was he going to launch into Act 2? Could he have picked a worse time for a mid-life meltdown? Men really have no emotional intelligence at all. Obviously, he had not picked up any signals from my voice. It was good that he didn't know that there was anything wrong. I would have a lifetime to fill him in about our girly day together. I could take all the time in the world to explain it to him. But, while I agreed with everything that he said, and in truth I was happy that eventually he had come to this realisation, could he not have picked a better day to air these thoughts? Not on Ruby's only day on earth. Though of course it was Ruby's existence that had brought on all this navel-gazing – and all that bloody travelling gave him far too much time to think.

"Luke, I am so happy to hear that – that you have made that decision."

But Act 2 was just about to begin.

"And another thing, Afric, I need to take this pregnancy stuff much more seriously. I promise, Afric, I will try not to miss any more doctors' appointments and definitely not any more scans. I will be there with you, holding your hand. At the next scan, I promise I won't rush out to feed the parking meter when it is our turn. I swear I won't be impatient any more and ask how much longer we have to wait in the queue. I swear I won't pace up and down, on the phone, glaring impatiently at you. I swear I am sorry, Afric, that I have not been more supportive. I have not been the ideal partner – I have not been much in the way of support. But that has all changed now, Afric. I am determined to be the best dad on earth. Please believe me that at last the penny has dropped. I now realise how lonely it must have been for you, going through all this on your own with no support from me. I have been so selfish, I realise that now. Please tell me that you forgive me, that it is not too late, and that you'll give me a second chance to be a good father."

"Yes, Luke, of course . . . you will be the best dad . . . someday." I turned and faced the glass box. "Luke, we have a lot to discuss when you get back, just you and me. We need to iron things out. We will sit down, be honest with each other, and we can work it out together. I guess the most important thing is that we still love and respect each other – that is all that is important – the other bits are only minor things – we can sort those out afterwards. Luke, I love you and I am sure that you will understand things from my perspective too. You are back on Friday, aren't you? Afternoon, is it?"

"No, it'll be the evening most likely. I'll be home for dinner – maybe you and I can go out to dinner, what do you think? Will we go out for an Indian?"

"Yes, that would be fine with me, Luke. We can talk then."

"Okay, let's do dinner – I'll book it."

"Look, I have to go now because we're about to go into another session. Bye, Luke."

I hung up and sat there motionless on the bed, glaring at our fate and our lost future.

There was a noise at the door. It was Jane. She peered through a small opening in the door.

"Are you all right, Afric?" she enquired gently.

"Yes, thank you, everything is just fine – or at least I think I'm okay. That was Luke. My husband. He doesn't know that we're here. He thinks I'm at an IT conference in Liverpool." I was desperately seeking her approval.

"That's fine," she said. "There will be plenty time to explain. Now spend time with your little girl and enjoy it. You'll only get one opportunity. It's fine, Afric, just fine. Concentrate on staying strong." She closed the door gently behind her.

She was gone. Now it was just me and Ruby again, and my turbulent thoughts.

I stood and walked back to the box. I looked into it and addressed my tiny girl.

"That was your dad, your dad calling from China. He was asking for you, asking for you and me. He

189

didn't know that today was your birthday, but when he gets home this time I will tell him. He'll be sad to have missed you but as I said it is for the best for everyone. You know, Ruby, in his own way and in his own time he'll grow to love something like you that is not perfect – in the end he will accept you. You see, sometimes it takes him time to accept things. But this time there was no time – they didn't give us any time. You and I had to do things so quickly, to organise everything, that we didn't have time for your dad to come around, so that is why it was just you and me. Oh Ruby, I do hope that you understand?" Gently I rubbed my little girl's tummy. I never did get to see her tummy, I never did open all those buttons on the babygro. I only opened just two buttons at the end of each foot, because I was terrified of what might lie beneath it.

"Now, where were we, Ruby? Oh yes, the picture. But, Ruby, Mummy is feeling a little tired from all the action today. I'm going to wheel you over here beside me so that I can have a nap. It won't take long – I just need about half an hour. And then when I wake I'll tell you more about the picture. Look, I'll put the picture in there in the glass box so that you'll have some company while I'm sleeping. I hope you don't mind if I have a little rest? Your mummy is wrecked."

Chapter 13

"Afric, Afric . . . sorry to wake you . . . you must be tired." Lucy was standing over me. Her eyes were soft.

I was completely disorientated. Had I been asleep all night or just five minutes? I looked around me, searching for a hint as to where I was. It had not been a dream or a nightmare, it was cold reality. I was still there in that room, the one with the cream walls, alone with Ruby in a private room of a maternity hospital in Liverpool. There with only my little girl in a glass box beside me for company.

"Afric, in the next while you will need to say a final goodbye to your daughter," Lucy said gently.

"Okay, Lucy, just five more minutes, just one last goodbye. I'm afraid I fell asleep." I was not trying to excuse my power nap, just trying to explain what had happened.

"That's okay, Afric – you need to rest, you need a lot of rest – no harm in cat-napping after such a long day." She rubbed the back of my hand to reassure me that it was okay, as if to say that I had not been neglectful of my daughter.

As she left I sat upright in bed and pulled the glass container nearer to me.

"So, my little angel, it's time for us to say goodbye."

I leaned into the glass box and picked up my daughter, the blue motionless bundle wrapped in a spotlessly clean white blanket. I held her tight against my chest.

She didn't need anything more from me. I was now redundant, a useless mother. She had come with her passport and she was staying only one short day.

"Ruby, my little angel, I love you. No matter what you look like you will always be my perfect angel. Take care, my sweetheart, and be good until Daddy and I come to get you one day. Henry and Penny will love you until then. Give my love to them both and tell them that we miss them, very much."

I folded the black-and-white photo in two, and folded it once again. I placed it snugly between the blue outfit and her pink raw skin. I didn't want her to be alone. The people in the picture would keep her company while her flesh and blood was on this planet.

"There now, you have your parents, all your grandparents and the aunties and uncles and friends with you so you won't be lonely. Go now, sweetheart, to your place where you can sleep for ever, a place where they will love you, where they love flawed people like you."

I pushed the red buzzer.

Lucy came in and slowly approached the Perspex box. She peered in as if check that all the contents were in order.

"Okay to go?" she enquired tenderly.

"Yes, thank you, Lucy – we have said our final goodbye." I smiled gently at her kind eyes.

I stood up, as though I was giving Ruby a standing ovation for performance. I wanted to escort my daughter to the door and out of the room. From there the lady with the kind eyes would look after her, and Henry and Penny would take care of her. She had come on loan to me for only a day; her final destination was elsewhere. She did really only have one day on earth because tomorrow, Wednesday, very early, they would take her to the crematorium. The lady with the kind face said: "They like to get the ashes back to Ireland as soon as possible." Thursday my little girl would be busy travelling. And on Friday we would be reunited – all three of us.

I walked to the door, and waved. I waved as she was pushed down through the cream-coloured walls of the corridor. Then they turned left at the end of the corridor. And she was gone, gone from me forever. There was no happy ending, like in the movies.

Alone, I sat on the bed and sobbed. The sobbing became howls, and the floods of tears ran down my cheeks onto my now defunct bump. I coughed and choked on my own tears. I cried myself to sleep. Then, the nightmares began: those torturous hours of restless sleep that were to become my new bed companion. Never did they disappoint. Nightly for months they visited my sleeping hours.

Chapter 14

A different lady with a sweet smile greeted me with a cup of coffee. "Good morning, Afric. Hope you slept well?"

I wondered if they had a factory attached to the hospital where they made all these kind people. It was as though they were all made with the same tender personalities and thoughtful ways. They all had full waists, slightly rounded faces and kind eyes – a very sincere type of kindness – you could tell that they really meant it. It was not just a job to them, it was a gift that they had and they were sharing it with those in need.

These people had a real job, I thought. This was not marketing fluff or consultancy drivel – it was a job at the coalface of reality. On a daily basis they battled with the certainly of death. I wanted to stay here forever, inside those creams walls. I wanted to be minded and cared for by this tribe of wonderful women. Life would be so easy with them around.

I looked up at the lady. Her gold name badge with brown lettering read '*Hazel*'.

"Thank you, Hazel. I did sleep well – for a while – but then the nightmares began."

I looked beyond her to centre of the room. I was hoping for a glass box, that it might have miraculously reappeared with a living angel dressed in a blue outfit peering over the side. The floor was empty. There was no box. My heart sank to meet my sick stomach.

"Nightmares are normal for the first while, Afric, and with time they will stop. Eventually they will fade . . . so too will the pain . . . it will ease . . . it may never go away but you will learn to accept it . . . you will be able to live with it. Afric, then you will be left with only the fondest of memories that you will cherish forever. It will get easier, Afric, just give it time."

She had moved to the edge of the bed, and the rough skin of her right palm rubbed on the back of my hand. She smiled gently at me.

"Don't be hard on yourself, Afric – give yourself time to heal from the inside out. The inside, you know, is the bit that takes time, plenty time. You will discover all the clichés are true, every one of them: time heals all wounds. But you will have to take that time." She stroked my hand again. "So you're leaving us today. You'll need to get up soon to make your flight – your file says it is at eleven – is that correct?"

"Eleven fifteen, I think – yes, it's eleven fifteen because it lands in Dublin at midday. What time is now?"

"It's just after eight thirty – so you still have plenty of time. We'll get you a taxi, Afric. Call me when you're ready to go, okay?"

Smiling, she left, closing the door gently behind her.

Hazel – well, presumably Hazel – had left a brown A4 envelope on the locker next to the bed. She had not drawn my attention to it – maybe she meant me to open it later at home.

I spilled the contents of the white envelope onto the brown cover of the bed.

There was a booklet and four tiny cut-out pieces: two hand and two foot prints. They looked like something from a kids' make-and-do class. I picked up the hand prints. They were so petite that they both fitted perfectly into the palm of my hand. Her hand was now inside mine, I closed my hand over her tiny little paper prints, careful not to crush them. I rubbed both foot prints. I was so proud of them, so proud of us, Luke and me, for getting something right: her tiny toes.

The booklet came from the same art class. It was like something from *This Is Your Life*. It had her personal details and her photos. They'd only needed two pages to record her short life. The foot and hand prints should have been part of her living body and not in a remembrance book that read: *Forever in Our Thoughts*. At the back of the book was a sleeve that held a clear plastic band. It read: **11.6.12 Baby Lynch. 10: 31**.

I gently touched the band; it was the wristband that Ruby had worn for her only day on earth.

Now my little angel, Ruby, was gone. Physically she had departed this world because of her troubled body. All I hoped now was that her soul would keep me sane. Of course that was the ironic beauty of it all: she was now tasked with looking after her mother. Luke and I were now parents of angel, a very exclusive club that no one wants to be a member of.

Carefully, I repacked the envelope, sealed it, and then got out of bed.

"Ruby, we are going home, to the room with the sea view. You and I are going home, our time here is done." I kissed the envelope and popped it into my pink-and-cream handbag. How cruel, I thought. Only a single brown envelope to remember my little angel by. The only evidence I had that she ever existed – other than my memories.

Until her ashes came home to us.

Chapter 15

"Just one bag to check in?"

"Yes, Dublin please, travelling alone, thank you," I replied. "Is there any chance of an emergency-exit seat?"

He looked from my face down to my bloated stomach and then back at my eyes. I wondered if I should say anything, but what could I say? 'Sorry, in fact you are wrong. I can sit in the emergency-exit seat because I am no longer pregnant.' Should I say that my inflated belly was only a farce and that it was only skin deep, that behind the skin was a vacant womb?

"Sorry, we don't have emergency-exit seats available – they are all booked up," he replied politely.

Thankfully, we had both been saved a difficult conversation.

I made my way to the boarding area.

My phone blipped, I stared at the screen.

Miss you, Afric, hope you survived the conference, very excited about the new job and coming home soon. Chat later, going to a meeting just now, hope all is well, Love you, Luke.

I sent a simple 'X' that would buy me more time before I had to speak to him. It would be easier to talk to him sitting at the desk overlooking Howth Head. It would be more restful there. It is easier to tell lies when you're in your comfort zone – mind you, I had done a pretty good job in Liverpool. I would be home and at my window in over two hours – one thirty at the latest. That would make it eight thirty in the evening in Beijing, a perfect time to call Luke. He would have done his pool swim and would be more relaxed. I would get home, shower, relax, pour myself a stiff drink and then call him.

The plane skidded to a halt.

I looked out the square window with the slightly rounded edges. The raindrops bounced off the tarmac at Dublin airport – they looked as though they were jumping up to greet the aircraft.

I began to relax. Very soon I would be home, sitting at the window. Knowing that I was not far from my comfort zone, my mind began to wander.

They say 'Trust your instinct', another cliché like 'Time heals all wounds'. Clichés had a reason to have been hanging around for so many generations. People use them time and time again, mainly I suppose because they are largely true.

But I had ignored my instinct. I deliberately had denied its existence – maybe because I was too scared to trust it. During those long six months of pregnancy, I didn't know that there was something wrong but I knew that there was something not quite right. I could never put my finger on it. I was unable to identify what exactly was the problem. Unable to recognise the issue, instead I chose to block it out.

Maybe if I had listened to my inner voice from the beginning this tragedy would have been avoided. If I had gone for an amniocentesis at an earlier stage of my pregnancy would they have discovered my baby's incompatibility with life? It still would have been very sad, but it would never have got to become this tragic.

Perhaps that was why I didn't tell anyone until I was over twenty-two weeks pregnant – maybe to protect myself from the imminent hurt. I had gone through the motions of congratulations. These now would be followed by a follow-up round of commiserations. That was what awaited me now, hundreds of well-intended empathetic condolences.

Inadvertently, I had been shielding myself from the pain, from the reality of the situation. Of this I was sure. It had not been the hormones that were making me feel sad for the past six months. It was my own body rejecting its own flesh, the very flesh that it had created. My body and mind were not elated because perhaps it was nature's way of protecting me from the deformity in my womb. It was preventing me from bonding with a child that would never survive outside the womb. I was saving myself from myself.

During those six months, I thought that I was going crazy, that I was losing my grasp on reality. I was relieved now that I knew it was my mind rejecting something that was trying to hurt me: it considered my daughter as a foreign body.

The raindrops continued to dance on the ground – there was something very therapeutic about it – it had a rhythm – there was almost a sensation to it.

"Miss, Miss, *Miss* – whenever you are ready – we need to get the plane clean – very quickly."

I wondered how long he had been trying to get my attention.

"Sorry, sorry, I was in my own world," I replied.

He smiled. Perhaps he could tell I was sad – you can see when someone is very sad – you can see it in their eyes. I smiled gently back.

I opened the large yellow door and climbed the threadbare stairs to the front door of the apartment. I was glad to be home. I poured a large glass of chilled white wine and sat down at the window.

The rain storm was slowly clearing, the dark grey mist had blocked out the entire headland of Sutton and Howth. There was no white-and-grey lighthouse visible, though I searched the sea for it. It must have finally toppled over and tumbled into the Irish Sea.

I took out my phone and typed: **At home, exhausted, going to sleep for a bit, will text later.**

Chapter 16

A Thursday in June, 2013

It gushed from between my fattened thighs; it drenched the bed sheets and soaked right through the mattress, leaving dark red circles in large patches. Its dark stained colour was all over my body, as though my body had been painted with large brushstrokes of red. I had been bathed in my own blood; it had turned my hair from dull blonde to brown. There could not be much left in my veins. My black nightgown was stuck to my skin.

My engorged breasts throbbed from the milk that was being produced; somebody had forgotten to inform them that they were no longer needed, that they were now obsolete. Like me as a mother. I was no longer required, I served no purpose.

But instead they produced and grew and grew, swollen and roasting. I wanted to pierce them with a knitting needle. Piercing them was the solution. I got up and walked from the bedroom into the kitchen. I reached into the top drawer of the sideboard. I fumbled around in the dim light until I found a kebab skewer. It sparkled – it was clean and unused. Perfect, I thought.

I retraced my steps back into the bedroom and then went through to the bathroom. I stopped at the bathroom cabinet mirror. I turned on the light over the mirror.

I aimed directly at my left nipple with the skewer. I punctured the faint-brown skin, tearing right through the nipple, right in the very centre. The yellowy grey gunge spurted everywhere. It was mixed with blood. This blood was a light red in colour. It was all mixed together. The milk and blood flowed from my breast. It had splattered everywhere. It was on me, on the walls, it stained the toilet bowl, the bathtub. I gazed back at the mirror. My face was stained with my own bodily fluids, and splashes of colours interrupted my freckled face.

Then ignoring the wounded breast, I refocused my attention. I took aim at the right breast. Again I carefully aimed the skewer so as not to miss, but I was not able to get the exact angle of the protruding nipple on the small bathroom-cabinet mirror. I opened the cabinet door, so that the mirror was nearer so as to perfect my aim. It was more difficult with the second breast as the bodily fluid that escaped after the first piercing had stained the mirror, obscuring my vision of my intended target. I tilted my head so that I had the perfect uninterrupted view.

I pierced myself a second time. This time I struck harder because the second breast was the more engorged and the more painful of the two. The stabbing needed to be fierce to stop my own body torturing me. If my body didn't know that it was inflicting pain on its own very being then I needed to act to stop the torture. I had to rescue me from myself. My own flesh was devouring my mind. It had to stop.

I was drenched in my own mess; it had managed to even grace my swollen vacant stomach with its presence. How sordid, I thought. It was as though the fluid was sneering at my bloated belly. I banged hard against my stomach, trying to instantly deflate it, hoping that the bloated bulge would disappear, that the hangover of a dead child would lift, that I would be relieved of a tragic death, that the nightmare would be over soon.

The puncture wounds in my breasts instantly relieved the pressure on my chest. The horror of self-harming had not yet been realised by my mind, only by my body. My body didn't care because it was so fucked-up and confused that it no longer could distinguish the different kinds of pain.

It was my mind I had chosen not to focus on – it was a much more complicated matter to heal. You can fix tits, I told myself. I remembered what the kind midwife had told me: heal from the inside out. That was what I was not doing.

I turned my head and saw him approaching. He wore a long coat. It was pristine white. He had a gold name-badge with dark brown lettering. I thought I could read the word '*Doctor*' on it, but he was too far away from me to make out his second name. It looked like it began with '*De*'.

He had dark-brown hair parted to the right; the fringe swerved over his forehead. He had green eyes, very green, the colour of olives. He had a button nose and, on closer inspection from where I lay, it was too small for his face. He needed something a size bigger to fit in with the contours of his head. His lips too were not full enough for his face. Everything seemed to be a size or two too small for his body and that included his neck. It looked as though they had just propped the head on his shoulders, like they had forgotten his neck – that they then suddenly remembered it and stuck it in at the last moment.

"Lynch, Afric Lynch, if you would like to come this way?"

He invited me to follow him into a room with a huge monitor with hand-scanners attached to it. He closed the door behind me and we were alone. I squinted to read this name badge. Its deep brown lettering read '*Doctor Death*'. I looked up at his olive-green eyes but his eyeballs had disappeared and were now replaced with sheets of shiny steel. His steel eyes gawked at me, as he smiled to reveal solid gold fangs behind his thin lips.

I sprang upright in the bed. I extended my arm to the far side, checking to see if I was alone. The sheets and my nightgown were soaking. I turned on the bedside lamp to my right. I forced open my eyes. I examined the dampness. It was not blood but a lather of sweat that had drenched my entire body.

The small grey digital clock read: **04:11 am.**

I reached for some water. I was completely disorientated. Panicked, I looked around me, desperate for a signal to tell where I was. I was relieved to discover I was in our bed and not in another room with cream walls, clear plastic tubes and large monitors.

The nightmares had started. The lady with the kind face had said they often happen. She'd said that often women relive the traumatic reality of losing a baby; she'd promised me that with time they would pass, that they would fade and some day they would disappear altogether. She said that I would dream again, happy dreams. However, she had failed to promise when this might be. For now, these nightmares would be my nocturnal bed companions.

I got up and had a cool shower. I stood there in the darkness as the water spilled over me, and thumped onto the bath's surface. The rhythm of the spilling water relaxed me. I stayed there for what seemed like hours.

Luke would be back in less than twenty-four hours. I still needed to work out how best to explain it to him – to clarify the reason for the deceit – why I had kept it all from him – why I had lied about Liverpool, about going to an IT conference for work. I needed to make it – the explanation – as painless as possible for him. Luke would want facts not emotions – well, at the start of the conversation anyway.

I wanted him to understand, to forgive me for keeping the truth from him. I wanted him to tell me that it was all okay now – that we were okay and that he would have done the same thing too if faced with similar circumstances. Unlikely, I thought.

But, most of all, I wanted him to understand that I was trying to protect him from our new reality, that I needed to protect him from himself, from his own sadness.

I was now afraid that the nightmares would reveal to him my total heartache.

I had just one day to work out how to tell him – so he understood. I felt almost criminal, as though it was my fault, as if I had caused our loss and pain. That it was my fault that our daughter was imperfect.

I looked down at my bloated belly. "Ruby, are you there, are you listening to me?" I had momentarily forgotten that my belly was empty. I looked from my belly to the ceiling of the bathroom.

"Ruby, how will I explain it to your dad? One of your dad's many great qualities is his attention to detail. You know, that is why he is so successful – because he reads the fine print, *all* the fine print – and when it comes to his dead daughter, he will want to know what every inch of her body was like – I will have to describe it all – relive all your imperfections for him.

"Ruby, do you think that he will blame me for it all? Will I be on the stand, on trial for our dead daughter's imperfections? I don't think that I have the guts for that. I could not now go through all that, all the blame. I think that my batteries have finally run out. So I will need to explain it all – properly and calmly – to your dad. He will want more of the detail and less of the emotions, so that logically he can understand all the different reasons that I did not tell him the truth. He will then assess the situation in a rational manner. And then with time – lots and lots of time – he can accept it too – someday – that we created a flawed child.

"Ruby, when I found out you were terminally ill, I decided that there was no room for anger or blame in my heart. So, what it is about is acceptance, grieving, and trying to stay strong. Then some time in the future, who knows when but eventually, it is about moving on. One day, eventually, we will get back to reality. Of course, Ruby, reality will be a different version from before, and that is fine too – I can accept a different version – but please, Ruby, send me some type of reality soon – some version for Luke and me to work with."

I stripped the bed of the sheets. In the low light I fumbled through the bed-linen press and located a clean crisp double sheet to sleep on.

I got back into bed, switched off the light. Maybe the nightmares might cut me some slack, I might get a few uninterrupted hours of rest, and I badly needed to rest. I drifted off to sleep.

My phone pinged and left a message from Swift Delivery: **Consignment Number AER33456/9 for overnight delivery has been successfully dispatched** from NHS Royal Merseyside Women's Hospital via London Heathrow, final destination to: Apt 1, Coliemore Road, Dalkey, County Dublin, Ireland. Please log onto our website to track your consignment.

By now I was fast asleep; the nightmares had taken the rest of the night off.

Chapter 17

A Friday in June, 2013

Today my little girl would come home; she was due home at the latest by four o'clock. Her dad was also due home today. I would have a full house this evening. I was looking forward to both their arrivals.

At two minutes past four I logged on to the Swift Delivery website and inserted AER33456/9 into the large white box on the right-hand side of the screen. I then pressed the smaller blue button that sat just below the consignment number. The website asked me to please wait, which I did patiently.

Very patiently. I stared at the screen.

Then in large black bold text a message appeared that read: **Consignment delivery complete. Consignment number closed off.**

My heart sank and I felt a sick sensation in my stomach. My head spun, I felt as though I would fall off the seat and crash to the floor. Where was my daughter? Had somebody taken her by accident? Had she got lost on the way home? Maybe she got lost coming off the boat or the plane? Maybe she fell off the side of a pallet and no one noticed? They must have made a mistake. They promised me she would be home today, before her dad got back. I dialled the Swift Delivery number in their Dublin depot; the nurse in NHS Royal Merseyside Women's Hospital had given me their direct line together with the consignment number. The Swift Delivery number rang out. Very slowly I punched in the numbers once again; maybe I had hit a wrong digit. It rang and rang and after what felt like a lifetime a clear-spoken male voice announced: *'Our office is now closed. Opening hours are from 9 a.m. to 4.00 p.m. Monday to Friday and from 10 a.m. to 3 p.m. Saturday.'*

There was no mention of any after-hours number or what to do in the event of an emergency. I googled out-of-office hours and Swift Delivery. Nothing of any use popped up on my screen. I could understand that the actual office was closed but surely the depot was open to receive and dispatch goods? If the office was closed, how then was I to receive Express Delivery service? That made no sense. I re-entered the dispatch number. I rechecked each digit. I was right – it was same as the number on my phone, the same number I entered the first time.

Again the screen read: **Consignment delivery complete. Consignment number closed off.**

I grabbed my pink-and-cream handbag, my phone and my keys and dashed down the stairs, out through the yellow door and the black creaky gate.

I opened the car door and sat into the driver seat. I punched **Tallaght Industrial Estate** into the sat nav. It took a few seconds to compute and then it said: '*Twenty-one minutes, in current traffic thirty-eight minutes.*'

I spoke aloud to myself, hoping to soothe myself with a composed tone. "Afric, stay calm. In just forty minutes you will be reunited with your daughter. It's just that there is a glitch in the system, some stupid random error. It's very simple. All that has happened is that your daughter has been delivered to the depot instead of our home, a very simple error. Now, Afric, we are going to drive to the depot and bring her home."

The sound of my own voice had a calming effect on me. I pulled myself together, then turned on the ignition. The radio blared as if screaming at me. Quickly I turned it off; I needed to concentrate on the task ahead.

I drove off in search of my little girl. I began to think how I might greet my daughter when I met her again, three days later. What should I say to my little angel, Ruby? I was passing time, trying to distract myself from the reality, repressing the fear that I would never find her again.

Well, I would start by telling her that I was happy to have her home, obviously. But that was not entirely true. I would be hugely relieved to have her home, but not happy to have her home like this, on someone else's terms and conditions. She was meant to be in a buggy with solid wheels so that we could jog up and down the East and West Piers, she was meant to peep out of the buggy and listen to me telling her stories about why the piers have two different-coloured lighthouses, one green and one red.

Where would I put her when I collected her? It was not like she was going to hop into the car and ask me how my day had been. She was, after all, in a freight package, so maybe it should go in the boot?

"You cannot put your daughter in the boot, don't be so ridiculous," I told myself. "Of course she won't go in the boot – you should be ashamed of yourself for even thinking that."

I looked at the passenger seat; I would put her there for the journey home. I tried to imagine her there, beside me in the front seat. I looked down on the passenger seat, back to the road, back to the empty seat and towards the oncoming traffic.

I would strap her in with the safety belt, and then she would be secure so that nothing more could happen to her. She would be safe there. She would be a little small for the seat, way too small in fact.

"Aren't there regulations about having kids in front seats?" I said.

Now that I didn't have Angel to talk to, I was beginning to find comfort in the sound of my own voice – it was like there was someone else there, someone talking me through the decisions.

You see, I was afraid with her being so tiny that she might slide off the seat onto the floor and hurt herself. I would take the towel from Luke's swim bag, the one he always left in the boot. I would wrap her in it so that she was secure and safe for her journey home. Otherwise she would look so ridiculously tiny, there on her own on the front seat. I would tell her that her dad would be glad that I had chosen his nice posh car to take her home in. I would say wasn't she lucky that she didn't have to travel home in her mum's car, her mum's crock?

Very soon my own daughter would be sitting beside me on that seat. According to the sat nav I was only fifteen minutes from the Industrial Estate where she would be waiting for me. I would have to ask one of the guys at the depot where they had her, because the reception area would be closed. I would take her in my arms and carry her to the car, I would concentrate on putting one foot in front of the other, I would count one two one two, and that would get me from the cargo pick-up area to the car.

In the car, she would not be in a child's car seat like she was meant to be. Instead she would be all wrapped up. I wondered how she would look. Would she have a huge label with a vulgar consignment number on her? How many times would they have written the code AER33456/9? Surely the box would be marked '*Fragile, handle with care*'? I imagined that it would be. Of course, I told myself, it must be. I mean, if you didn't describe someone's charred body as fragile, what would you classify as delicate goods? I hoped that they would handle her with care, that they would not just toss her around or bang her off things. Of course they wouldn't mean to hurt her – it was just that they wouldn't know what she was. You see, if they tossed her about, she would stick to the inside of the box. I thought it better if all the ashes were together in a pile. It would be more organised like that. Otherwise she would be as disorganised in death as in life, with all the bits mixed up, and I didn't want that. I wanted her to now be at peace.

Maybe when she first got in I would say nothing for a while. I would just look at her. I would want her to feel very comfortable, at ease, to relax after her long journey. Sure there was plenty time to settle in, there was no rush. We would have a lifetime to talk, to work it all out, and to explain things.

After a while I would ask her was she angry at me for leaving her all alone in Liverpool? I hoped that she didn't disapprove of me for going away and leaving her with the lovely nurses with the kind faces.

I would ask her daddy if he was angry with me for leaving her all alone, because maybe he too would be cross with me. That would be two people that I loved cross with me, my daughter and my husband, and right now that was two too many.

I would ask her: 'Were they kind to you, sweetheart? Did they treat you well?' Well, of course all the lovely nurses with the kind faces would have treated her well! 'I am so sorry that you had to come home on your own.' I would tell her that it was not what I wanted either but that there was no other option. 'I hope that you weren't too lonely on your own, were you? Were you scared, were you? Was it very dark inside the box?'

Then I realised that I had no idea how she had got back to Ireland. What a terrible mother I was, not knowing how my baby got home – how utterly careless of me. Maybe fate was right – maybe I was not good and kind enough to be a mother.

"But, Ruby," I said to the vacant black passenger seat, "it's not important how you got here. This time it is not about the journey, it is more about the arriving. All that is important is that you're safe with me now. Ruby and Afric together now and soon Luke will be here too. He'll be happy too to have you home, even though he won't really understand it all at the beginning. Later he will, though – I am pretty sure."

Other commuters had perfect kids sitting in their compliant child seats. They looked at me sympathetically as the tears poured down my face and onto the steering wheel. I could barely make out the road through the tears. How nuts must I have looked, sobbing uncontrollably and talking at an empty passenger seat?

I looked from the road to the empty seat, and then back to the road. Yes, on the way home I would definitely lock the door of the passenger seat. I mean, just in case – what if someone tried to steal her? Not meaning to take her, of course. They would not mean to steal my dead baby, but they might think that the package was an iPad or an expensive smart phone that had come from the States. God, what a shock they would get, to have robbed a parcel and to find it was a box with a pile of ashes!

I slammed on the brakes. "Oh Jesus!" I spluttered out. "Jesus, Afric, that was a pedestrian crossing! How the hell could you not have seen the large white markings on the road?" I spoke to myself aloud, hoping to shock myself back to reality, to the here and now.

A very heavily pregnant woman waddled out onto the road. I glared at her, wondering how I would have looked if I had ever got to full term with my tiny angel, Ruby. Would I have had a rounder bump, or would it have been flatter? Maybe it might have been smaller, more compact, than this woman's? Would I have carried the bump higher up or lower down my stomach?

Some women suit pregnancy, I told myself, they wear it well – others just don't get it, it doesn't suit them, and they don't suit it – it's as if they're not getting along with their bump, like it gets in their way so they never look terribly happy about it. I most definitely had come under this category, the uncomfortable group. The lady with the bulging stomach didn't look anything, neither ecstatically happy nor dreadfully sad – she just looked pregnant and going through the motions.

She looked at me as she continued on her way across the road. Now she was directly in front of me, only the windscreen of my car between the two of us.

I stared at her with envy. Suddenly, I wanted to be her – bloated and pregnant.

The tears welled up in my eyes. I was sure that she could feel my piercing eyes on her plump body. No doubt she thought me some crazy creepy weepy lesbian ogling at her bump. I put on my pink sunglasses so that she could not see my watery eyes.

I would discuss with Ruby what room she would like to sleep in. I would ask her 'Would you like to be in your own room? The room that your dad painted for you?' I would tell her that he painted it white because we didn't know if she was going to be a boy or a girl. I wouldn't say that I told him it was a really boring colour for a baby. He had insisted, and when Luke insists it's best to let him have his way. Anyway, I didn't really mind, but if our little girl didn't like the colour we could change it to any colour she liked – well, I mean, within reason.

Then it struck me that I was being silly, because I had forgotten that my baby would be asleep all the time, so she wouldn't need to be in a bedroom – she'd just need to be somewhere nice, where she'd be happy. Some safe place so she didn't get lost any more.

"Anyway, Ruby, I don't think that we should put you in the baby's room. I think that it might be too lonely for you there – you probably wouldn't like it there. You might be lonely there in the dark, though I guess it doesn't get much lonelier than it is in that package."

Yes, I mustn't forget to ask her was she scared in there, on her own on the way home.

Would my little girl like to be able to see the sea?

"Ruby, would you like to look out over Dublin Bay, onto the lighthouse in Howth? If you were at the window then you could see all the boats passing, you could see the ferries bringing all the tourists in – you would have a great view from the window. Yes, the window with the sea view would be the best place for you – that is Mum and Dad's room and that way you would be with us. Well, kind of with us anyway, safe behind the large bright yellow door in the apartment with the high ceilings and cherry-coloured walls.

I would ask her what she thought. Of course, I would tell her that there was no pressure and she could wait until we got home to decide then – when she saw the place – that there was no huge urgency to decide now.

A big blue-and-yellow truck quickly brought me back to reality. He had overtaken me on the outside lane and then cut in ahead of me, forcing me to slam on the brakes. I hooted at him but he paid no attention to me.

"Jesus, Afric, honestly you are going to kill yourself and probably someone else today unless you bloody concentrate. Cop yourself on." This time my tone was a lot firmer.

If she came as Express Delivery, then she most likely came by plane, she most likely came as cargo. She would have come in the belly of the plane, with all the suitcases and with all the happy people coming home from their holidays. I was not happy with the notion of my daughter being flung around an aircraft, bumping into suitcases and boxes and sticking to the inside of the box.

I couldn't believe that I hadn't asked one of the many ladies with the kind faces how my daughter would get home to me. It had completely escaped my mind that Wednesday morning.

Ruby must have come in over Dublin Bay – she would have been like contraband in the belly of the plane – not allowed in this country.

She would have passed all the swimming places that Luke and I never got to take her to. I would tell her again that I did take her to those swimming places, when she was alive, when I was pregnant. I would tell her again that I used to swim from the Forty Foot to Bullock Harbour and that I would talk to her on the way, dreaming about her swimming with her dad and me – a little girl dressed in a coloured wetsuit, swimming between her mum and dad.

Those dreams had now become my nightmares. I had lost my dream, my dream of a little daughter.

"Please, Ruby, I am begging you to tell them to take away the nightmares, to take them away forever, and to give your mum some peace."

I looked from the empty passenger seat back to the road.

"So, my little girl, we would have put you in the middle, between the two of us, between your mum and dad. That way we would be able to protect you from the jelly fish so that they couldn't sting you. We would be able to see them and we would guide you away from the man o'war jellies. With Mum and

Dad on either side, we would scare away the great big seals that follow us sometimes when we swim. I wouldn't let the seals frighten you the way that they terrify me. Sometimes when we swim a large bristly face pops up beside us and is glaring us in the face – it is terrifying. Once when your dad and I were out swimming a large grey seal's head popped up beside me. I thought it was your dad and then I realised it was a seal. I screamed and screamed and the seal just stayed there in the water and looked at me. I swam towards your dad and the seal swam beside me. That evening your dad and I sat overlooking Dun Laoghaire pier, giggling. I think that your dad was genuinely upset that I confused him for a seal.

"You know, it's sometimes occurred to me that maybe the reason your dad and I got on so well together back then was because we swam together so much and we couldn't talk when swimming. We swam all over the world together – we swam in Cuba off white sandy beaches fringed with palms and turquoise water, we swam through shoals of multi-coloured fish in Egypt. Then, in the evenings, we would get out the Maxi Memofish guide and identify the fish, the turtles and the coral that we'd spotted that day. We would spend hours arguing about what we saw so we didn't have to talk about anything else. You see, Ruby, we saw the same fish because we would hold each other's hand and with our other hand point out the marine life. We would stay in the water until our skin tingled from the salt and the sun. Eventually, we would drag ourselves begrudgingly from the sea when the skin on our fingertips was so wrinkled that it looked as though it was a few sizes too big for our fingers."

The sat nav interrupted my story in its slight American twang: '*Four minutes to your final destination.*'

Chapter 18

My phone rang. It was not a number that I recognised. The area code was for Dublin.

"Is that Afric Lynch?" a male voice asked as soon as I picked up.

"Yes, yes, it is – how I can help you?" I responded rather sharply. I was terrified that some cold-calling sales person was going to clog up my mobile as I desperately searched for my daughter's remains.

"This is Swift Delivery here. I have a consignment for you. I have to apologise. There's an error notice appearing on your tracking number, saying that the consignment has been delivered – which is wrong – it's not, I have it here in the van with me. You see," he continued, eager to explain, "some bloody gremlins got into the Express Delivery System, which means when someone looks on the computer to look for their package, they receive a wrong message. For some bloody reason they're receiving a message saying: 'Consignment delivery complete. Consignment number closed off.' So, missus, I really apologise. Sure isn't the reason most people use this online service to be able to trace their delivery, so that they don't have to spend all day home waiting for their package. Now, Áine . . ."

I didn't bother to correct him.

". . . can you tell me what your consignment number is and your full name and address?"

"Just one moment, please – can you please hold for a second – I'm driving."

I indicated to move into the left lane. A huge haulage truck whizzed past me as I tried to manoeuvre the car onto the left shoulder and the car vibrated as it went by me. I hated this bloody monster of a car! What in the hell did he need a car this bloody size for, just for the two of us?

The car ground to a halt on the hard shoulder.

"Are you still there?" I asked eagerly.

"Yes, I am, I'm here."

"What do you need? An address, is it?"

"Yes, your postal address and the consignment number that you received from the person that sent the consignment, if you have it handy?"

I grabbed my phone. "Right – the consignment number is AER33456/9, the address is Afric Lynch, Apartment 1, Coliemore Road, Dalkey, County Dublin."

"Thanks . . . A-f-f-rick . . . I think that I just rang your doorbell. I think I'm outside the house. Is yours the one with the large bright yellow door? You see, I came here directly from the airport and stopped here first on the way to Bray. God, isn't it a great day to be –"

"Oh no, you're not at the apartment, are you?" I interrupted him mid-sentence.

I didn't know whether to be furious with him for the mess-up with the delivery or to thank him profusely for having brought my daughter home.

"Yes, I am."

"Well, actually I'm on the way to your depot in Tallaght. I'll be there at the depot in a few moments. I thought that maybe the consignment might have been there, so I rushed out to collect it – so I'm not home."

"Sorry about that, missus, sorry for the mix-up. I'm really sorry, missus – there's a problem with the bloody system today, as I said. Can I leave the package with one of your neighbours? Is there someone that I can get to sign for it, someone nearby that might take it?"

I froze. I was speechless and horrified at the thought of leaving my precious package with some random neighbour that I didn't even know. They would just sign for her and then fling her into a corner, not giving her the respect she deserved. Now that would hardly be the proper welcome home for my daughter, to be left with someone that she didn't know – bad enough that she had to travel all that distance on her own. Worse than that, her mother did not know how she got back to Ireland. Jesus, what if Luke asks how Ruby got home? And now the delivery man, unintentionally, was making my daughter's homecoming sound so transactional.

"No, there's no one that can sign for it." My voice had begun to shake. I took a deep breath, steadied my voice and said: "I am the only person that can sign for it."

There was silence on the phone. It was a potential standoff between him and me. The man whose name I did not even know.

"Well, missus, I'm not sure what we can do in that case, if there is no one home."

"I can wait here at the depot until you get back," I offered, eager to find an instant solution. You will be coming back here to the depot?"

"But, you see, I have another package to deliver to Bray so I need to go there first, before I come back to the depot. You see, there were three express deliveries that came in on a flight from London this afternoon."

The thought of my daughter moving farther and farther away from me, when she was just outside the house, began to upset me. "Is there nothing else you can do, to get my parcel to me?"

"Well, missus, I could try to deliver it again on my way back from Bray – that would be in an hour or so."

"I don't know, I don't know, maybe . . . will it be safe till then, do you think?" I enquired anxiously.

"Of course it will be! I have it here beside me on the passenger seat," he said, sounding a bit offended. "Sure 'tis only a small box, well wrapped up, all sealed with Sellotape. It has 'Fragile, handle with care' written all over it, so when I saw that, with nothing in the back of the van, I put it here on the seat beside me. I didn't want it banging around in the back and getting damaged." He was clearly happy with his logic.

"You won't leave it unattended, will you, at any stage, do you promise?" I asked, my voice quivering.

"No, missus, no, missus, it will be as safe as houses with me, I promise."

He sounded puzzled. He had obviously tuned in to my desperation.

I couldn't bear the thought of my daughter sitting in the passenger seat beside some stranger. I squeezed my fists hard until my nails hurt my palms. I stared directly ahead. This time there was no stopping the tears; they streamed down my face.

"What's your name?" I managed to ask between stifled sobs.

"Michael is my first name. Michael Thompson," he replied.

I took a deep breath and sobbed, "You see, Michael, that is my daughter that you have in that brown package. That is my little angel that has come home to me. Those are her ashes in that box, so please be very careful. That is why you must not leave it with the neighbours. I must have that package – it's all that I have to remember her by. I want my baby angel back with me, not with some stranger. I'm afraid that you will lose her. Please be careful, very careful with my little Ruby." Somehow through my sobs I had managed to get it all out, to get my desperation and heartache across.

"Ah, *Jaysus*, missus, I am so sorry, ah fuck, that is terrible, fucking terrible, sorry, missus, I didn't mean to swear – that is shocking, just shocking, I am so sorry, so sorry. What do you want me to do?" His thick Dublin accent was full of emotion, his voice lower now, softer.

I could tell I had ruined his Friday.

"Are you there, missus, are you there?"

"Yes, I'm here," I sobbed gently.

"What happened to her, missus? I hope you don't mind me askin' n' all?" His tone was gentle and soothing.

"She died, she was sick – she had a fatal foetal abnormality, she was incompatible with life – there was no hope – no future for her – and she died in Liverpool. So they put her in a box and sent her back to us. That was the only way of getting her home to us – with Swift Delivery. So my little angel girl came home in a box all wrapped up and all alone."

"Is your fella with you, missus? I mean, are you on your own? I don't mean to be askin' personal types of questions, but I mean is he with you now? Is there someone with you now? I just want to know you're okay?"

Eager to assure him I would be okay, I replied, "No, he's away on business but he'll be back later today."

"Right so, Áine, sorry, it's not Áine, is it? 'Tis an unusual type of a name, what is it?" He was clearly rattled by now.

"Afric, my name is Afric, like the continent. Just take the A out of the Africa, the last A, I mean, and you have it: Afric. Though it has nothing to do with Africa, in fact." I was happy to finish the conversation on a more positive note.

"Right so, I'll do the other delivery out in Bray and stop on the way back. You'll be home by then, won't you?"

"Yes, yes, I will."

"I'll make it as quick as I can – I'll be back in about forty-five minutes. I'll give you a shout when I get back."

"Thanks, thank you, Michael, and take care of my angel. You won't leave her alone in the van, sure you won't?"

"No, missus, I won't. I'll take good care of her. She'll be safe with me."

"Good, good, see you very soon."

I hung up, weak with relief. My head flopped against the head-rest. I tilted the rear-view mirror, so I could see my eyes, and with my middle left finger I gently removed the mascara stains from my lower eyelids. I had got made up to greet my visitors.

My phone flashed. It read: **two missed calls**. I pressed the centre button and it read **Luke**. I pressed it a second time and again his name popped up. I stared at the screen, stunned for a few seconds, still trying to compute the conversation with Michael.

No need to call Luke, I thought. He was just doing what he used to do when we first met. Back then, he would call from London and say: "Two hours and I'll be in your arms, holding you." It used to make it my heart flutter – it made me all gooey inside. But today was not the day for this. I had less than two hours to locate my daughter, get home and prepare myself for Luke's arrival. And rehearse my pitiful explanation.

I was also terrified that he would pick up from my tone that there was something seriously the matter. I chose not to return his calls.

My mind flitted back to the conversation with the Swift Delivery man. He must think me terrible, an awful person for abandoning my daughter in Liverpool, I thought. What kind of a mother would allow that to happen, to let her innocent daughter travel home all on her own? What would he tell his wife that evening? Of course he would tell her, of that I was sure.

I bet that in future he would wonder what was in every box he delivered. When he saw packages the same size and weight as Ruby's, he would wonder if they were another heartbroken woman's child's ashes.

The wife would get it. She would explain it to him, and she would explain that Ireland is not the place to have a fatal foetal abnormality, that a woman in Ireland is forced to see such a pregnancy through to the bitter end. She would tell him that the baby had no chance of survival outside the womb, that it was incompatible with life. She might say it was sad that the girl had to go to England – and then come home and have to tell lies – she might say it was not Christian – and she might say 'And, you know, Michael, they probably wanted that baby more than winnin' the lotto.' I was sure if she was Michael's wife she was the salt of the earth.

I wondered if he, Michael, had ever heard this term 'incompatible with life' before. She would work it out for him and then, when they thought they had all the elements of the story, they would proceed to judge me. Decide then whether they felt sorry for me, if what I did was right and wrong. Would Michael still feel compassion for me after he had spoken to the wife? Maybe like most humane people he would feel even worse for me. Maybe he too would be furious with the system, with the country, maybe he would think that it is terribly inhuman, a cruel place to live, not only corrupt but brutal too.

At least he'd have a new story for the pub. I pictured him with his mates. I visualised him as a measured decent man. He would sit in the same spot in the same pub where he was part of the furniture. He would maybe have three, at the very most four pints. The same men would always sit in the same seats in the same area. I thought that maybe tonight he might opt for the four-pint option. I wondered how he would communicate the story to the lads. Would it be through a series of interconnected grunts, like a series of short statements but when all knitted together they tell a story? Or would there be a prolonged address to the gathered men? All huddled and drooped over a pint of Guinness, would he tell a heartfelt story about a woman and a box that came in the post?

I hoped in my daughter's honour that he would tell a compassionate account of a heartbroken woman frantically looking for her daughter's ashes. Would they deduce from the story the barbaric nature of this godforsaken island? Then of course there would be an intense debate – or maybe not. Would there be an increase in grunting, or would the mumbling just be faster than usual, or be more joined-up than usual?

Or maybe it might all be too much for them and they would sit there in stony silence. Yes, maybe silent nodding would happen, without any grunting or mumbling. They might just sit there in total silence, a silence like when you honour the dead.

Then they would all look toward the telly in the corner to save them from this emotional minefield. They would be saved by the repeat of an earlier GAA match. They would all order a fourth pint, by way of condolence, a way of showing solidarity, and they would all head home eventually to their respective wives, safe in the knowledge that such a topic would never be allowed airtime again. Their wives would ask them if there was anything new in the pub, and they would mumble something below their breath – no news, they would respond. They would have been in the dangerous perilous land of emotions, a place where the average Irish male would never want to visit.

I had to compose myself. I wiped the tears from

inside my pink sunglasses so that they were no longer steamed up. I blew my nose very hard as if trying to rid my body of my sadness. I punched in **Coliemore Road** and turned his car around.

Chapter 19

I looked at the digital clock on the dashboard. It read: **16.33**. By five thirty I would be safely reunited with my daughter. I took the M50 that headed south; I would leave the M50 at the Blackrock exit.

Luke would be home later. I would need to muster up as much courageous energy as possible for him.

Would he rush in to hug me? Would it be at that moment when he pulled me tight against him that he would learn about the loss of his child or would it be sooner – would he know at a first glance? What would I say, what should I say? I wondered if he would ask for the details immediately. Of course he would. His first question would be simply what, followed by how and then why – why didn't you tell me? I would have to tell him, straight away. He would want to know every detail of what actually happened. I understood this. He would be devastated by our loss, utterly devastated, because underneath the perfectionist, he was a big softie, behind those islands of freckles was a good kind man, trying to do the best for his family and if that meant long stints away, then that was what he had to do to deliver the goods.

As I drove along the M50 I admitted to myself that Luke was the one who had been more excited about the pregnancy. It had always formed an integral part of his life plan. I was much less enthused about expecting our child. It was not so big on my agenda and I had adopted the philosophy that if it was meant to be it would happen. This irritated him a little but he was careful not to comment on it, for fear I thought that he was pushing his own agenda, which I did.

I was pregnant for him. I had hoped that a little person in the house might eradicate his tendencies to slip into deep sadness. I had hoped that he might forget those dark times, that a third person in the house would be a distraction from his melancholy.

But I hadn't reckoned on my own melancholy. All the people supposedly in the know said that "the blues" were connected to the hormones. I didn't care to count how many people had told me not to worry, that it was a "just the hormones" and that it would pass. The dreaded hormones only raged during the first trimester, they insisted. They said that the blues would pass along with the morning sickness. It would all pass and then I would be blissfully happy – "blooming" they all said so confidently. But the only blooming I was, was going blooming crazy.

I knew that both our families whispered, in hushed tones, that I ought to feel lucky to be pregnant at my age. "Imagine not being grateful to be expecting in her early forties," they muttered. That was the problem with women these days, those people thought, too much focus on their career and other interests like travelling and seeing the world and before they know it is too late, too late for the eggs. The eggs they muttered about sounded as if my organs were on sale in a supermarket. The manner in which they mumbled made it sound like my eggs might just go off like those in the shop. I knew well that was exactly what Luke's mother thought and I found it mildly entertaining that my mother-in-law was so ridiculously blatantly obvious about it all.

So I patiently waited for those torturous three months to pass. I ticked off each one of those endless ninety-one days meticulously. Each night before I fell into bed, sick, exhausted and demented, I would draw a large black X on the calendar. This exercise illuminated the long and dark tunnel that had become my daily existence. The twenty-ninth of March was technically the last day of the first trimester; I had marked it in red, with a happy smiley face beside. I only had to make it to that date – from that date on the calendar miraculously it was all going to get better, to change. I was going to be transformed into some type of a rounded motherly earth figure with fattened hips and bloated boobs, or so everyone told me. I looked forward to this total transformation with great anticipation.

Those early days of pregnancy had been filled with sharp words, the outbursts quickly followed by lengthy silences between Luke and me. Then the guilt would set in and he would apologise for upsetting me. I would blame myself, and then we would argue as to whose fault it was. It had become a vicious circle.

Before the pregnancy we had always held each other in the highest respect but now that all-important reverence seemed to be dwindling. I felt like everything was under threat: our high opinions of each other, our marriage, both our sanities, and my pregnancy. I knew that there was something not quite right, but I could not quite describe it.

I didn't know myself any more; I didn't recognise myself or my own actions. My own being, my own body and mind, were completely alien to me. I no longer believed my own feelings. How could it be that my own basic instinct no longer existed? It had abandoned me, leaving me lost and helpless. I was truly scared of myself, unsure how I might react. I no longer trusted myself. I never knew how I might respond to situations. I had become erratic and emotional. I even found myself a nightmare to be around. I disliked my own company; I wished for days when I could escape from myself. I was not at all happy with this person I had become. I felt possessed and trapped within my own flesh and blood.

During the last six weeks of those torturous three

months, Luke travelled even more than usual. Though I never said anything, or accused him of doing so, I guessed it was to be away from the hell that was our relationship. He had tried to be loving and caring, to go that extra step for me, but he was consistently greeted with abrupt and curt replies. Soon, he stopped bothering to try. He obviously concluded that the easiest way to not bother his wife was by not bothering to be home. Time differences between China and Dublin helped to avoid those screaming matches down the phone. No doubt he thought that after the first trimester he would travel less – we would work it out – after all, it was only the bloody hormones – it would pass, or so they told him.

The blues never did lift, I never did blossom, and I kept my pregnancy a secret up until the twenty-second week. My work colleagues could not understand why I didn't announce my due date five minutes after discovering I was pregnant. Instead I concentrated on concealing the truth. I managed to successfully continue the denial by dressing appropriately. I was proud of myself to have got to twenty-two weeks without telling a sinner other than Luke. He did think that this was a bit strange, but as he had learnt over the past twenty-two weeks, better to say nothing, so he remained silent.

I was right. There was something wrong. Something fatally wrong. I was carrying a baby that was irreconcilable with life. These genetic abnormalities were lethal mistakes in development. Now I know it was my instinct protecting me, shielding myself from my own being. I now wonder was my extreme despair nature's way of preventing a bond forming between a mother and her terminally sick baby. My baby had been alive but not really present. Was my misery in some way going to become part of my ability to accept that I was never going to have a healthy happy child? In retrospect, maybe it all formed part of the acknowledgement and acceptance process.

The phone chimed and vibrated on the dashboard, startling me out of my acknowledgement of these home truths. I glanced to the left of the steering wheel. The phone's scratched screen read: **Sue calling**. I reached to the dash and picked up the phone. Overstretching, I pulled the steering wheel to the right and swerved into the middle of the road. A black Toyota Corolla coming against me hooted at me – he delivered a filthy look as he whizzed past. I moved back onto my side of the road.

"Sue, Sue, are you there? Just give me one second – the hands-free is not working and I nearly killed someone – hold on there for a second – I am just going to pull into Seapoint Beach."

"Afric?" Sue didn't seem to register my earlier comment. "What the hell is going on? Are you okay? I just had Luke on the phone – he is trying to contact you – he's demented trying to contact you – he's so bloody worried, he was in tears on the phone. Is everything okay? Are you okay – are you and the baby all right?"

"I know, I know, I'm going to ring him now – I had a few missed calls from him – I'm driving and couldn't call him. I will just now." But why was he so frantic? Just because I didn't answer a few calls?

"He asked me about Liverpool – he asked if I knew anything about what happened at the hospital in Liverpool," Sue said then.

I was struck dumb. How could Luke know anything about what had happened in Liverpool?

There were no words to explain my lies, well, no words now for Sue. I would need to save the explanation for Luke – he was the one that deserved the first one of these. I suspected there might be many more rounds.

I looked out onto Seapoint Beach. Early-evening bathers splashed around, a pudgy-looking dad held his little boy by the left hand as they jumped over the low waves. I could see Howth Head in the background, the yellow furze cheering up the green headland.

"Is there something wrong, Afric? Is everything okay with you and with the baby? Has something happened, hun?" The tone of Sue's voice was urgent but caring. "Luke said he had no phone – he lost the charger and has been using his iPad since Wednesday – but he plugged in the phone just now and one of the text messages was . . . Afric, what happened in Liverpool?"

"What was the text message, Sue, what did it say?" I said, surprising myself with my almost detached question.

"He said one of texts was from NHS Royal Merseyside Women's Hospital – he read it out to me, Afric – he's distraught, he's pacing the floor, he's sick with worry, he wants you to call him, to talk to him, to tell him what is going on."

"But what did the text say?" I repeated my question to Sue.

My phone bleeped, announcing the arrival of another text message. Maybe Michael was back in Coliemore Road with my daughter, I thought. I would need to go now and ring him.

"Afric, I can't remember the exact wording but something about a transaction of NHS Royal Merseyside Women's Hospital . . . nearly two thousand pounds on your joint credit card . . ." Her voice trailed off.

I froze. I glared at the sea as if waiting for an answer. I looked at the clock at the bottom left-hand side of the sat nav: **17.01.**

"Afric, please go home to Luke, won't you? He's really frantic."

"Home? Oh God – oh no – fuck, are you serious – no, please no – no, he can't be home."

"He is, Afric. He phoned me from there."

"Oh, God. Okay, Sue, yes, I'm heading home just now. Tell him . . . tell him . . . I will be with him in a few minutes. Sue, will you call later? Please? In a few hours? After I have seen him."

"Afric, tell me you're okay?" Sue pleaded.

"Yes, yes, I'm okay, I'm fine. But the baby, our little girl Ruby, she was sick, too sick and she did not make it – she was not meant for this world." My voice began to tremble as I struggled to stop the tears.

"Oh God, Afric . . . Go home, Afric, go home to Luke. I am going to call him now and tell him you'll be home in a few minutes – you will, won't you, Afric?" Sue voice was softer now, a few tones lower.

"Of course, of course I will," I replied and she hung up.

I opened the car door and allowed the warm summer air to fill the car. There was a faint whiff of the sea. I longed to be in the water, there doing the lap of Seapoint Beach. I wanted the cool Irish Sea to take all this pain away, to sweep it all out to sea, to bring back those happy carefree days of sea swimming, of being in love. It was the carelessness of it that I craved. The tide was coming in and the yellow buoys were drunk again, with Dun Laoghaire pier in the distance.

l looked back at the screen: **1 new message and one missed call**.

I pressed 171. A male voice told me that I had one new voicemail, left on Friday at 16.42. I held the phone to my ear and listened intently. I expected it must be Michael.

The pudgy middle-aged man and little boy jumped over the waves. The boy was a miniature version of the man. They both tilted their heads slightly to the left as they guessed where the next new wave would break. A brown-and-white Jack Russell had joined in the action. It was not clear if the dog was theirs.

There were a few pink, yellow and white-coloured heads cruising in different directions – they were further out to sea. In the background, the DART whizzed past, packed with early Friday-evening commuters. The sunshine twinkled on the windows of the dirty train, greatly cheering up its drab appearance.

"Afric, Luke here, just got home on an earlier flight – sorry, my phone has been dead since I left China. I am here in the apartment and no sign of you. Give me a shout when it suits. I have great news, the promotion came through. No more trips to China. Happy days! Oh, someone at the door, must go, maybe it's you without your keys. Hope it's you!" He hung up.

I turned on the ignition, indicated and pulled out on to the sea road, in shock. I was acting like a zombie. What was Luke doing home, how did he get home so early? How was that possible? His flight wasn't due to land until after six o'clock. I had to get home, now, right now before Michael arrived, with the consignment, with the package that was our dead daughter, with Luke's little dead girl called Ruby that he knew nothing about.

I put my foot to the accelerator and whizzed in the direction of Dun Laoghaire. I had dressed up for Luke's return, made a bit of an effort. I wore a long floaty black cotton dress. My silver sandals were wrapped around my ankles and snaked up between my large toe and second toe – they had a bit of a Greek look and feel to them. My reddish-brown hair was neatly tied back, tucked in at the bottom of my neck. I wore my pink sunglasses on my head – they acted like a hair-band, keeping the shorter wisps out of my eyes.

The sat nav read: **Thirteen minutes to destination.**

The phone read: **1 new message.**

I opened it.

Luke Lynch has signed for consignment AER33456/9.

I felt sick to my empty stomach. I swerved towards the right-hand lane. I opened the message again so I could reread it.

It still read: **Luke Lynch has signed for consignment AER33456/9.**

"Oh fuck, what now, what am I going to say to him, what if he opens the package, what if he discovers the truth that way?"

I gripped the steering wheel so tightly that the white of all ten of my knuckles were on show to me. My heart was racing, my head was dizzy and my legs felt lifeless. I was afraid I might just pass out there and then in Dun Laoghaire, right next to the East Pier.

What if he opened the parcel there in the middle of our cherry-coloured living room with the sun flooding in and discovered that all his dreams of the future were now nothing more than a pile of ashes in a box? I knew him – he definitely would never recover from that – I was sure that we would never ever come back from that. Luke would feel betrayed by me, my betrayal would then start the blame game, and I knew how that would end.

What was I to do? Should I ring him and tell him not to open the parcel until I got home? That I would explain everything when I got home, just not to open it for the moment, until we were together? That I knew that he had the parcel, my parcel, well, addressed to me but the contents were soon to be ours? What should I do?

Or should I ring and tell him what really happened now, before I got home, tell him the whole story so that he would not be quite so shocked and upset when I arrived?

I was afraid to see the sadness creep into those Dairy Milk Chocolate eyes. Would that dreaded mist creep in and steal him from me? Would sadness engulf him once again?

Panic started to set in, my mouth was parched, I could not think clearly. My heart started to thump inside my skin, and I thought I might vomit onto the steering wheel. My hands could barely grip the wheel, they were so damp. Would this be the final straw in our marriage? Would he blame me?

And I'd have to tell him right at the start when I saw him. Explain to him, like the doctor had to me, how we had created an imperfect person. Our chromosomes together had got it wrong; our own bodies had got it wrong, so wrong that it was fatal. Our own flesh and blood together had created that fatal mistake. Our own beings had inflicted this pain on us three. Would I tell him how I saw our fatal mistake dead before my own eyes? Would I say that I was very sorry that we had created something that was incompatible with life?

Would he want endless rounds of tests to pinpoint exactly where the problem lay – or would the results of the amniocentesis be sufficient? I would hand it to him to read – there it was in black and white – the result – Patau Syndrome.

Would he surprise me and accept it – accept the findings, resigned to the fact that we were that unlucky statistic, that one in ten thousand, which you never think you might be? Maybe he would understand.

The reality was that I didn't know how he would react, because I was not sure I knew Luke any longer. We were out of touch with each other's minds, just like we had both tuned out of the life we had once enjoyed together.

I began to take long deep breaths; I concentrated on the road and on my breathing. I inhaled deeply through my nose, held my breath for three seconds and slowly expelled the air through my mouth. Slowly and methodically, I repeated the exercise.

The lady with the slight twang spoke out loud at me: '*In current traffic you are five minutes from your destination*,' she announced.

This time I took a longer, deeper breath, and my shoulders almost rose up to meet my head, I inhaled so furiously.

I pressed the centre button of the phone. The screen read: **new message**. I selected his name – **Luke**. The fingers of my left hand tightly gripped the back of the phone, and with my thumb free I typed: **Please**

don't open the package. Home in a few minutes. I added two Xs and then quickly deleted them. I replaced them with '**Afric**'. It felt more apt.

If he threw me out, I would go to my mother's place. My mother had been very supportive during all this and would completely understand and accept the situation. Lizzy got it, she would understand without judging, she would also see his side of story.

I calmed myself again. *Why* would he react irrationally? He was not an unreasonable person. The person I had married just two years ago was a level-headed, calm and logical person; I must remember that. The baby was not my fault. It was a combined botched effort. Together, Luke and I had got it wrong. If he did attack me, I would tell him that it was a joint effort, that he was as much to blame as I was. I would then explain that really there was no one to blame. I would tell him that and he would be okay with that. In this instance, no one was right, instead we were both wrong.

I expelled what felt like the remaining air from my lungs. I loosened my grip on the steering wheel and colour returned to my knuckles.

I indicated and turned down towards the Forty Foot. I pulled in just before the steps that led down to the water's edge. I needed to gather my thoughts, to get myself together. I needed to talk to Michael to find out what had happened, what he had said to Luke and how Luke had reacted about the package.

I could wait; I could wait another five minutes before I opened the package, before I got home to find our box of grief, the remains of our charred dreams. This box of grief would be with us forever, for a lifetime. What was five minutes in a lifetime?

Luke would understand the problem that I faced – of course he would understand the syndrome that Ruby had after I explained it to him. Patau Syndrome to me by now had become a household name like Fairy Liquid Original, but to Luke it would not have the same familiarity, just yet. The baby had some physical features that resembled a child's and a few organs that had kept it alive, like a powerful heart. But Ruby, our little Ruby, was incompatible with life. I would explain to him that she would never have survived outside the womb, that there was no hope to be had. That was simple to explain, to anyone. And that was the reality, whether he liked it or not. Now, our reality was our imperfection, an imperfection that we together had created.

I searched through received numbers and redialled the number beside 16.22.

He answered immediately. "Swift Delivery, Michael Thompson speaking."

"Michael, I was speaking to you earlier this afternoon – you have a package for me."

"Yes, Áine – Áine, isn't it?" he replied, proud to recognise the caller.

"No, Afric, Afric Lynch," I replied, a little irate. "Michael, do you know what happened to my package, the delivery for Dalkey? I thought you were going to take it to Bray and then deliver it on the way back – isn't that what you said?"

From the wall of the Forty Foot, I could see a bunch of scrawny youths in oversized shorts. They hugged their knees against their underdeveloped chests, and threw themselves carelessly into the calm blue sea. As they plunged into the water they howled, then frantically they splashed their way back to the steps, emerging from the water a shade whiter than before. They repeated the exercise over and over again.

"Agh, missus, great news, great news altogether." He had by now given up on tackling my name. "After I spoke to you, while I was parked up in front of the gate, a fella with spiky hair and a face full of freckles frightened the bejaysus out of me. He tapped on the passenger window. You know, I was just getting over the shock of talkin' to you n'all. So I rolled down the window and the fella with a foreign accent asked me if I was trying to deliver to Apartment 1, the upstairs apartment, just now?" He paused. "Are you still there, missus?"

"Yes, yes, I am – what did he say?"

"Well, I told him I was Michael Thompson from Swift Delivery. I told him that I had a consignment for Afric Lynch, that I was just talking to her and she was on her way back now to sign for it. And then, the fella, your fella said 'I'm her husband Luke Lynch' and he offered to sign for it, so that I didn't have to come back again. To be honest, missus, I found his accent a bit like hard to understand. He said he didn't want to bring me back on such a lovely day, I think that is what he said. Then I told him what I told you, that I was going to do a quick delivery to Bray and that you, his missus, said that you was the only one to sign for it, that's what I told him. I told him that I would keep it safe until it was delivered to you. I told him that I had promised you and that I was a man of my word. I dunno if he understood what I meant."

I could tell from Michael's tone of voice that he wanted to be praised for doing the right thing.

"Your fella muttered something about shoes, but again, missus, I could only catch half of what he said – something like you need more shoes when you're pregnant, bigger feet 'n all. He seemed in a kind of rush – he said he had just got home early from somewhere and he needed to shower. He said he would sign for it. Then he got a bit rattled when I asked him to show me some ID. I told him it was company policy, not my policy. All the time I was remembering what you told me about keeping the package safe. I was only doing my best. I told him that was what big companies were like, all bloody rules . . ." Michael's voice tapered off. "I said to him about a household bill, to get one with both your names and then I could give him the package. He seemed a bit annoyed but I didn't care – I had given you my word, so he came back down with one, a bill addressed to Mr and Mrs L Lynch and his driving license. Then he signed the form and I gave him the small brown-paper package. He thanked me, told me it was a beautiful day, then missus I thought about saying sorry for your trouble, but the words just would not come out. I dunno what happened but I lost me voice. Then he went back in through the yellow door, and that was it. Is that okay, missus, is it?"

"Thank you, thank you, Michael, for getting the package safely to me – thanks."

"Not at all, missus, and sorry for your trouble."

Michael was gone.

The kids had by now tired of the entertainment of flinging themselves off the rock. The summer tide was filling up quickly and early-evening bathers arrived with their worn towels rolled in a ball and tucked under their arms.

There was another text, another from Luke: **Please Afric please come home, please come home and tell me what happened. Tell me you are okay, that is all that is important.**

I drove along by Bullock Harbour. As the tide was incoming many of the boats with the painted names were out fishing, gone to get an evening catch, and the harbour looked sad without them.

Now, I imagined Luke in the apartment pacing the beige carpet in a circular motion, talking to himself, calming himself for my arrival, awaiting the news, the Liverpool news whatever that might be. He would be looking out of our bedroom window onto the pavement below, sitting or standing there, waiting and watching for the car, for to me to arrive. I guessed he would have looked out at Howth Head and onto the lighthouses, maybe for some guidance, desperate in search of an answer, scolding himself, blaming himself for whatever went wrong, though he was not quite sure what it was yet.

By now he would have convinced himself that the credit-card authorisation text he received was just an error. He would have called them, I guessed. Now he probably would be talking to some guy in a call centre for Amex in a third world county. Being incredibly polite and professional but firm, he would tell them that they had keyed in a wrong digit, he would tell them that it could easily happen to anyone. He would assure them that when they are sending literally hundreds of thousands of credit-card text confirmations for security reasons mistakes would happen.

I pulled the car in below the window of the apartment. I lined up the back wheel perfectly against the pavement edge, on my first attempt. I could feel the glare of his accusing eyes from above, from the window. I did not look up.

I took the keys out of the ignition and reached across to the passenger seat that was empty: on it was only my pink-and-cream handbag. I reached into my bag and took out my phone. It read: **1 missed call.**

It would have been from him. I placed the phone safely away into the side pocket of my bag. Then I zipped it shut. It was too late now for chat.

I began to walk slowly away from the car, towards the apartment. My footsteps crunched on the gravel. I climbed the stairs slowly and gently opened the door to the apartment. I walked into the hall and through to the living room. I dropped my handbag on the cream carpet next to the blood-red sofa, below the high cherry-coloured walls.

There on the table was the brown-paper package and an A4 document. Beside them were three tiny yellow babygros with elephants on them. They would have come from China. He would have chosen yellow, not knowing if it was a boy or girl, and because yellow in China is considered an important colour. It symbolizes good luck, it is considered a prestigious and beautiful colour, it is held in high esteem.

I walked to the table, and very gently with the tips of the fingers of my left hand I caressed the rough brown-paper packaging that was covered in clear Sellotape. Its contents were marked '*Fragile, handle with care*'.

I picked it up in both hands.

Then I heard the chair of my desk, the one in our bedroom, creak. I turned around. Luke was standing in the doorway, staring at me.

"Jesus, where the hell have you been? I've been worried sick about you, out of my mind worried. I don't know how many times I've tried to call you – I even called Sue – what has happened, what is going on? Afric, are you okay? What's the matter? Is the baby okay?"

Slowly, I placed the brown-paper package back on the table. I walked towards him and into his arms. He held me tight, very tight. He gave me one of those bone-crusher hugs.

We held each other so tightly that I feared my blood might stop. I lay my head on his chest. I was in his arms, in the safest place in the world.

I pulled back a little from him and looked in his eyes.

"I am so sorry, Luke, so sorry. Our baby is gone, she is gone forever. She was very sick, she would never have had any life, she would never have lived. They told me she was incompatible with life, that she would never live outside the womb."

I could see the growing horror on his face.

"I'm sorry I couldn't tell you. I had to do it, to do it alone. I didn't want to hurt you. That is why I went to Liverpool, just me and her so that we didn't hurt you. Please, please, forgive me. I was trying to protect you from yourself, from those dark moments. I didn't want those sad times to take you from me too. I could not bear to have lost you both. Please understand."

I held his face firmly in my hands and looked into his deep chocolate eyes.

He pulled away from me. "Oh no, Afric, not our little baby. No, please don't say our future is gone. That is all I have ever wanted, our own flesh and blood – say it isn't true, Afric?"

Then he howled and howled like a wounded wild animal. His wails had a familiar ring to them – they were just like the ones that invaded my mind and body four days earlier. I knew his pain, his sadness and disbelief. His howls, after what seemed a lifetime, turned to gentler sobbing and I reached out and held his face cupped in my hands for a very long time, as with my thumbs I tried to dry the tears that rolled down his cheeks.

"Shh, Luke. Shh, Luke. She was very sick, too sick for this world," I whispered. I traced my index finger along his lower lip, over the freckles, and kissed him tenderly.

"Afric, I am so sorry. I am so sorry you had to do this alone, sorry I was not there for you. Afric, you are my world. I love you to bits."

Then, he wiped the tears from my cheeks and kissed me tenderly on the forehead.

We held each for a very long time, until our limbs hurt from hugging each other. My tears soaked the black hairs on his chest; they hung there like dew on a winter's morning.

I took him by the hand and led him to the living room.

"Luke, it is time to meet your daughter, to meet her for the first time. She is beautiful, so beautiful – it's just that she was not for this world. You know, the nurse said she looked like me, that she had my cheekbones but she definitely had your long legs. She got the best bit of us both. She was really fucked up but so beautiful at the same time. Will I tell you all about her one day on earth? We both did the best we could. She wore a blue outfit with an elephant on it – oh Luke, our daughter was so sick!"

Then I took him by the hand and led him to the kitchen. I picked up the large kitchen scissors, and went back to where the brown-paper package lay.

Carefully, I cut through the Sellotape and layers of brown-paper packaging and through the consignment number.

There, beneath the high ceiling and crimson walls we held each other once again, only this time with a solid wooden urn between us. We hugged one another so hard that the corners of her box dug into our flesh.

The dark handcrafted wooden box had a gold plate that read:

Baby Ruby Lynch
Died 11th June 2013
Rest in Peace
CW00013506

Our daughter had come home to us. We were now parents of an angel, called Ruby. Ruby was now in her own box, not in a glass one like at the hospital. She would stay in her own box now, there on the mantelpiece like some ornament that you might bring back from your holidays and admire.

From there she would watch over us, forever.

The End

Acknowledgements

To Paula Campbell for taking a gamble on a controversial novel and for your terrific support, and great guidance. To all the staff at Poolbeg for all their hard work. To Gaye Shortland – for your endless patience, dedication and unending hours of editing.

To the staff in Holles Street Hospital for your great care. To the foetal medicine team in NHS Liverpool Women's Hospital for their outstanding medical attention, kindness and support. To my great friend Ethna Murphy who guided me tenderly through the heartache of early child loss – I can never thank you enough.

To our kind work colleagues and tremendous friends – thank you all for your amazing support during a very sad time.

Maeve, I am so sorry you never got to see the book – or a book! My lifelong dream of being snuggled up beside you on a bookshelf has finally come true. To Gordon Snell who doled out – in double quantities – his and Maeve's encouragement, love and support during the past year. To my Uncle Kevin – you better be looking after my daughter up there!

For all our family, Gary's parents Kay and Grahame, our brothers and their partners: Daniel, Derek, Brian and Brendan, Janice, Naomi, Honor and Dani.

To my amazing parents Dan and Joy who have been a tower of strength, hope and love – always, but especially this year – who believed when they got the letters from the Australian outback in the nineties that I could write – despite it taking time and inspiration to get going.

To my husband Gary Smith (*not* Luke) who I adore to be with – you are the best thing that has ever happened in my life. Nessa and Paul, thanks for introducing us!

This book is a legacy for our beautiful angel, Zeldine Binchy Smith, much wanted but too imperfect for this world. This book is for you.

Interview with the Author

To what extent is this book based on personal experience?

The loss of my daughter Zeldine was the inspiration and motivation for writing this book, and my experiences during that traumatic time form a large part of the novel. But it is a novel – it is fiction not autobiography – and I have manipulated events and depicted relationships in a way that gives it a more dramatic structure. Choosing to write it as a novel allowed me to pick, choose and invent as I pleased. So, for example, though the character of Luke is fiction, as are the marital problems between him and Afric, the sea-swimming is not – my husband Gary and I have spent endless hours sea-swimming side by side. My amazing friends, wonderful family and my privileged months of travelling in Europe, South America and Asia have all found a place in the story. I hope that these dilute the tragedy and sadness of the novel. Those parts were of course easier to write about because they flowed and made me happy. The story about falling out of a chemical toilet in central South America is totally true! And goes down as the most embarrassing story of my life. Although I have clocked up quite a few more!

You started this book at the beginning of June and sent it to the publishers mid-September. How did you write it in such a short time frame?

Well, after Zeldine came home to Ireland at the end of May, I decided to take the summer off to give myself time to come to terms with our loss, to get my head straight and so that Gary and I could spend some time together. God, if you were to pick a summer to recover from a fatal foetal abnormality, didn't I pick the right year? The hottest summer on record ever!

I had started a different novel in 2007, then had an early mid-life crisis, gave up my job and headed off travelling around South America on my own. I came back, changed jobs, fell in love, got married and tucked the novel away safely in the hope that one day I might come back to it. Last May I dusted it down and restarted it. I thought it was good – but it didn't flow – maybe because I was not in the correct mind-frame to bang out a happy-go-lucky romantic tale in the snow . . . so I shelved it once again.

Then, one beautiful day after Zeldine had come home, Gary and I bumped into a delivery guy trying to find a house near where we lived. The conversation was very similar to the passage included in the book. I asked him was he Michael, the Michael who had brought Zeldine's ashes to our door two weeks before, and he said yes. He sympathised with us both and said how sorry he was. Gary and I then went swimming at the Forty Foot and on the way back I told him I was going to write about Zeldine for the summer. We put a desk into our bedroom at the window with the view over Dublin Bay, Howth Lighthouse and the cherry tree, and I began to write. So *Ruby's Tuesday* was actually inspired by the incident of meeting the 'Swift Delivery' man.

I sat down and literally wrote from early morning until late in the night. I did take breaks – I walked with my friends, swam at the Forty Foot and Seapoint, jogged and drank white wine – after all, as I kept telling Gary, I had six months of white-wine-drinking to make up for. But for the most part I sat at the window with the street view and seascape and banged out the novel.

Some days I had to give myself an emotional break and I would write then as if I was numb. It would be totally detached writing – like the episode where Afric drives around Dublin with her daughter. Then other days I would sob gently, and others I would howl with the painful memories. Some days the writing made me happy – especially when I was writing a funny scene – and I would roar laughing, remembering the madness of my single reckless days.

So, seated at the window, I banged on the laptop, reread, rewrote and then rewrote again – I was like a possessed woman.

Then in mid-September I was due to go back to work, so my deadline in my head was to submit the book before I went back. I had adhered religiously to each one of the different agents' and publishers' guidelines. I got up very early that Thursday morning, a blistering Thursday in the middle of September, and sent it off to two agents and two publishers. As I jumped on the DART on yet another amazing sunny morning I felt a huge sense of relief that I now had a legacy for my daughter, that she would not just be in a wooden urn with gold writing, that she would have a book dedicated to her – whether published or not. This was something I had done for her – Gary and I.

Silently, I hoped and prayed that I would never hear from the agents or publishers again. As far as I was concerned I had done my bit. But one agent came back and thought it would be good as an autobiography, another as a chunkier novel – less intense.

And then on a Saturday morning in October – Paula Campbell from Poolbeg called and said that though it needed work they wanted it – in the style and format in which it was written. I cried and cried – tears of happiness, relief – I guess proud that a lifelong dream might possibly come true. Now, looking back, I think I cried because I was so terrified – that it was now real – the book. My novel was going to be on the shelves – and my dream of being published – our dream of a legacy for our daughter – had nearly come true.

The sea plays a large role in the novel. Obviously it is important to you in real life?

I have a great passion for the sea and spend a large amount of my time sea-swimming. But I didn't grow up by the sea. Instead we spent our summers swimming in the water tank at the back of our house, having Olympic Diving and synchronised swimming competitions. The tank was filled with frogs and the odd water rat, and so much slime that by the end of the summer you could not even stand on the bottom. Health and safety was not a priority in those days – especially as the supply of water for the tank came as a milky-white delivery . . . compliments of the local dairy! Dad had a friend who knew a fella who worked as a milk-truck driver. The driver would wash out the milk truck – or so he told Dad – after a long day of delivering milk to the co-op. Then he would refill it with water and drive it to our house – to 'the water tank', as he called it. I would correct him and tell him it was the 'swimming pool'. The man had a fat yellow-and-faded-green hose extending from the back of the truck that just reached our swimming pool. Every year, he said: "Aren't ye lucky that the hose just reaches as far as the tank?" Every summer before he arrived I would worry that the hose might not reach that year – or that he might bring a shorter hose by accident. And then the summer would never begin. Dad and the milk-truck driver would go the conservatory and have a chat and a drink. We, the kids, would watch the white-coloured water trickle over the freshly painted bumpy walls of the inside of the tank. The cobalt-blue paint seemed to glue the tank together and acted as a concealer for the unwanted vegetation that blossomed on its walls. We called that green vegetation 'coral'; it was not precious, just not to be touched. We would sit on the edge of the 'pool', asking every five minutes "Is there enough water to get in yet?" The man would reply, "Nearly, very nearly – it'll be full soon" and we would smile back politely. To fill the swimming pool took three hours and we sat there, afraid that the entire summer might pass us by, and that the disfigured walls might drink our milky water. This man was the dream-maker – once the tank was full of milky water the summer holidays had begun! But the last five minutes were a whole lifetime out of that creamy water.

By night we would fill the swimming pool with water from the kitchen taps – we smuggled it out in little glasses – ever fearful the water would disappear through the cracks or the sun might take the water away. And then the summer would be over.

So, yes, water, swimming, the sea, always played a huge part in my life. And the sea had a powerful influence on this novel. I would sit there for hours and hours in the blistering sunshine, tapping away, and whenever I was stuck I would write about Dublin Bay and describe a waterscape. I would write about the lighthouses – they always seem to give me some kind of guidance, other times inspiration when I was stuck – then the words and tears would flow again.

How did you manage to write during such a sad time?

As I said before – it was a release – beneficial. It was definitely part of the healing process. It was an outlet. It allowed me express my sadness and disappointment, it allowed me to document the fact that I was not crazy and losing the plot, it explained my ambivalence towards the idea of being a mother.

As an author, I suppose there are two ways of motivating yourself: do you tell everyone that you are writing a novel – thereby nearly mortifying yourself into finishing it – or do you tell no one? I suppose it depends on your personality. For me, I wear my heart on my sleeve so the hiding away approach would never have worked. I told the world and his wife that I was writing a novel about a woman who had a fatal foetal abnormality – and sure the men never again asked me how the novel was going – a win-win result for all!

How do you feel about what happened to you?

People have asked whether I feel angry that it happened to me – angry that I had to be that statistic – that one in ten thousand. I suppose the honest answer is no. I felt a lot of emotions but anger was not one of them. It isn't even a year since Zeldine's birth and death – so maybe that emotion is still to be discovered – there is still plenty time in which I could be angry. But I think: at whom and why? Such things are a part of nature – no one's fault. I live in the first world – so I got time to grieve, to deal with the pain, to go back to work at my ease – I'm not sure it would have been such an easy situation in a less advanced society. Though God knows Ireland can hardly be called 'advanced' in this respect. I suppose that every society in the world has its serious flaws. They too make a country what it is. Political, social and economic diversities are often what inspire artistic creativity of every type: the flaws of this country have inspired my novel.

Have you always wanted to be an author?

In short, yes – I always wanted to. I suppose I was greatly inspired by my cousin Maeve Binchy and my dad, Dan. Maeve did really believe that everything in the world was possible – attainable through hard work and dedication. She never had the notion that you had to be amazingly creative to succeed to be an author – you had to be creative of course but it was as much about dedication and hard work as creativity.

When I was younger and wanted to write I didn't have that total dedication and discipline. I seemed to struggle with my style back in 2007 when I started the skiing novel. It was a love story set on the slopes in Austria – boy meets girls and happy-ever-after ending. I was busy having a great life and my discipline back then was not as good as it is now. Then I fell in love and sure that takes up time – a lot of time –

making him fall in love with me and then with Ireland was in itself a full-time job!

Have you ever had anything published before?

Yes, I had a 300-word article published in the *Evening Herald* as to why investing in skiing gloves was essential if you were going on a skiing holiday! It was a tiny article but it was a start. Then there was a long gap to 2013. I sent a few travel articles to the broad sheets about Oman and South America but none of them saw the light of day. My dream job was to be a travel journalist. It's an extremely attractive and yet a very difficult world to break into. It was a dream from early on. Just after I finished college I spent six months in the Australian outback – up in the Northern Territory outside Fitzroy Crossing, mustering cattle and working as a cow girl and cook during the mustering season. I wrote a lot up there. Every evening, after sitting around the campfire and chatting, there little else to do – so I wrote describing the screaming sunsets, the locals and their traditions, wrote about mustering. I sent those letters home and at the same time kept a very detailed journal – so yes, I have always dreamt about writing in some way.

Much of the book is written in quite a humorous

style. Did you adopt this style for a purpose or did it just come naturally to you as you told your story?

Well, I think I am by nature an upbeat humorous person so, yes, it did come naturally to me. But I was also conscious of the fact that the humorous slant on things served a purpose. The subject of the novel is dark and painful, but I didn't want to deny the more joyful side of life or depress my readers too much! Some of the most serious scenes in the book, though heartbreakingly sad, are normalised by touches of humour and other times they are wrapped up in an entertaining style, like when the sonographer is scanning the baby looking for the cerebellum.

The warmth and kindness of many of the people depicted in the book also serve to keep it from being too dark.

I think in the end, in a bizarre way the story is uplifting and that is how I wanted it to be.

Do you have any tips for aspiring writers?

I suppose a lot of writing is about discipline: staying at the desk when the words don't flow, writing through the blocks, avoiding the cul de sacs when you take a character nowhere and have to delete your way back up the path and onto the main road again – I seemed to do a lot of that.

One point is that while it may seem easier at the time to write in the first person, it blocks out lots of options such as introducing other characters – and at times it can really limit style options. It took me a lot of time to get this so I spent many hours down dark writing cul de sacs. One of the many good things about a great editor is that they can help you to work that bit out – or more importantly work that character back in – they help with the road blocks!

Another great tip – one my dad gave me and I think the most important bit to remember – is to "write forward" – don't go back and read yesterday's words – instead start with fresh words on a blank page.

Set yourself a goal, particularly if you have a deadline – I aimed for 3,000 words a day – but always ensured I did 2,500. I would count the words on an hourly basis and subtract it from 3,000 – it was huge motivation – and a frustration – but it made it attainable. And if on a Friday I did not have fifteen thousand words I would work the weekend – write for seven days.

Another point: Maeve always said, "Don't write slow – the writing is no better" – so, bejaysus, I wrote like a demon – obsessed with getting the words on the page.

Most important of all is to bloody stick with it – even when you think the story is crap and you really doubt yourself. When I was really stuck, sometimes I would jump to another chapter – a section that might be easier to write. I would say it is about fifty-fifty. Fifty per cent creativity and fifty just hard slog – like a good administrator. I think the key for me was *not to leave the desk* – I had to write through the pain and self-doubt. The key is to keep going – and I think that is what makes it so therapeutic.

So why did you really write this novel?

To help me and in some way to tell the story of early child loss. It is my story and the story about the decision that I made – it is not intended to be self-help guide or the A-Z on fatal foetal abnormalities. It is to plant in the reader's mind the thought: what would your decision have been? Would you have chosen to carry your daughter to full term – knowing that she would survive at most probably hours– or would you have chosen the options of a termination for medical reasons? What would you have chosen faced with a child that is incompatible with life? The novel does not seek to judge – it merely poses the question – nor does it seek to answer it.

This contemporary novel addresses many modern-day issues, not only Irish current topics but issues that women all over the world face, like some women's ambivalence towards maternity, the tragedy of being told that your child is incompatible with life, the reality of early child loss, the challenges of stabilizing a marriage after such a tragedy.

Ultimately, it is a novel, and one that I hope readers will think is well-crafted, suspense-filled and, though sad, a treat to read.

So do you believe in life after death?

I believe when people die their souls don't just disappear. They are up there looking after those that they loved. Those people I loved and cared for are now looking after me. On tough days they help me make it through. It is like having a safety blanket up in the sky. You can talk to them – any time. I find it great company. These daily conversations do my heart good and entertain me endlessly. It's an intimate relationship that only I am privy to.

On great days I thank them, and on other days I tell them that I need guidance. I find that really comforting. It is a fantastic feeling to be alone but never ever to feel lonely. It is a strange sensation but it takes in every way the fear out of living. I guess when you lose someone dear to you, you then understand the pain. It is the worse pain in the world but you know now what to expect painwise the next time – so it takes fear out of losing someone else.

I don't believe in a higher or better being. I am not religious. I believe in good souls – who love, guide and inspire you.

Discussion Topics
for Book Clubs

The Story

1. What is the significance of the title? Would you have given the book a different title? If so, what would your title be?

2. What were the themes of the book? Do you feel they were adequately explored? Were they brought to life in a cliched or in a unique manner?

3. What did you think of the structure? The style of the writing?

4. Do you think first-person narrative was the right choice for this story?

5. What scene was the most pivotal? How do you think the story would have changed had that scene not taken place?

6. What scene resonated most with you personally in either a positive or negative way? Why?

7. Has anything ever happened to you similar to what happened to Afric in the book? Did you react to it differently?

8. What surprised you most about the book?

9. How important is the setting and time period to the story? How would it have played out differently in a different setting? What about a different time period?

10. Were there any particular quotes that stood out to you? Why?

The Characters

1. What motivates the actions of the characters in the story? What past influences are shaping their actions?

2. What are the "dynamics of power" between the characters? How does that play a role in their interactions?

3. How do the roles of the various characters influence their interactions? (That is, for a woman: roles as mother, daughter, sister, wife, lover, professional, etc.)

4. Do you disagree with the choices of any of the characters? What would you have done differently?

The Ending

1. Do you think the ending is appropriate? How would you have liked to have seen the ending turn out?

2. How have the characters changed by the end of the book?

3. Have any of *your* views or thoughts changed after reading this book?

4. What do you think will happen next to the main character?

Overall

1. Are there any books that you would compare this one to? Does this book compare favourably to them?

2. What did you learn from, take away from, or get out of this book?

3. Did your opinion of the book change as you read it? How?

4. Would you recommend this book to a friend?

≡ WARD RIVER PRESS
titles coming 2014

AVAILABLE NOW
The Friday Tree by Sophia Hillan

COMING SPRING
The Last Goodbye by Caroline Finnerty

Sing Me to Sleep by Helen Moorhouse

COMING AUTUMN
Into the Night Sky by Caroline Finnerty
The House Where it Happened by Martina Devlin
Levi's Gift by Jennifer Burke

BOOKS TO READ, BOOKS TO TALK ABOUT